Sailor Take Warning

The Painted Lady Inn Mysteries

By

MK Scott

Books by M K Scott

The Talking Dog Detective Agency
Cozy Mystery
A Bark in the Night
Requiem for a Rescue Dog Queen
Bark Twice for Danger
The Ghostly Howl
Dog Park Romeo

The Painted Lady Inn Mysteries Series
Culinary Cozy Mystery
Murder Mansion
Drop Dead Handsome
Killer Review
Christmas Calamity
Death Pledges a Sorority
Caribbean Catastrophe
Weddings Can be Murder
The Skeleton Wore Diamonds
Death of a Honeymoon
Cakewalk to Murder
Sailors Take Warning

The Way Over the Hill Gang Series
Cozy Mystery
Late for Dinner
Late for Bingo
Late for Shuffleboard
Late for Square Dancing

Chapter One

THE ROUND, GOLDEN sun glistened in the pristine blue skies rather like a Christmas ornament, except it was May. The low hum of the waves, punctuated with an occasional childish scream of joy as a child met the ocean for the first time, provided background sound. The Victorian mansion was encircled by a white wrought iron fence. Donna Tollhouse, innkeeper, and her sister-in-law Maria stood on The Painted Lady Inn's wraparound porch while peering in the direction of the ocean, which would have been visible if the trees hadn't leafed out so much.

"I could help with your regatta-themed dishes," Maria offered with a grin.

There were a few more screams, not so childish but equally as playful. Donna, who had been holding Baby Cici, her niece, cut her eyes to Maria and asked, "Did they hire another half-dozen hot lifeguards this year?"

"Oh my!" Maria rolled her eyes and waved her hand in front of her face as if the thought heated her up. "You should see them. I doubt they'll be here long. Most probably aspire to be models or actors."

"Well then," Donna began, then cast a mischievous glance behind her where her husband was seated in one of the wicker chairs, reading the local newspaper. "It's been quite a while since I've taken a stroll on the beach."

Mark lowered his newspaper to reply, "I'll be more than glad to take a walk on the beach with you. No reason for you to join the mob of Legacy women drooling over boys young enough to be their sons."

A derisive snort erupted from Maria. "There's a female lifeguard, or maybe two, attracting all the old geezers' attention."

Leave it to Maria to go for the zinger. Even though she knew her husband was teasing about the lifeguards being young enough to be her son, the fact it could be true nettled her some. Sure, she'd never see fifty again. Since she'd married late, she'd never have children, either. The fact weighed on her as she played with her niece. Getting married and having children always seemed like one of those things she had plenty of time left to do—until she didn't. She consoled herself with the thought she wouldn't have been a good mother with her exacting tendencies.

Baby Cici took that moment to yank on the chain holding Donna's readers. The beaded chain broke, sending beads pinging and spinning across the porch. Her glasses had the good fortune to fall inside her shirt.

Maria held her hands out to take the infant. "Cici! Look at what you did."

The baby laughed and cooed with pride as if destroying the chain had been her objective. At the grand age of eleven-and-a-half months, Cici was pulling up on the furniture and making tentative steps, much to the delight of her adoring fans. Unfortunately, her beginning efforts at walking were not only wiping out the various knick-knacks scattered around the inn but had also put a rip in one curtain. Even the inn's unofficial puggle mascot, Jasper, was startled when he was inadvertently used as a stepping block, helping the curious toddler reach a tabletop.

From Donna's position on the porch floor, she swept up the errant beads into her hand, considering Maria's earlier comment—not the one to see the hot lifeguards, but the offer of assistance. "I appreciate your offering to help."

Her sister-in-law's delicate laughter reminiscent of wind chimes sounded. "But?" Maria said and lifted her eyebrows as she shifted her child to the other hip. "I hear what you're *not* saying. Whatever I might do doesn't balance out what havoc your niece might do in the meantime."

"I didn't say that." However, Donna may have thought it. "I didn't think Tennyson did much when he was here, but surprisingly, without him here, I'm stressed trying to get everything done."

Before her sister-in-law could reply, Donna held her hand up. "I've taken care of the matter. I put an ad in the paper for help. Even got a few calls about it. One candidate sounds ideal. She's coming by soon. Of course, you're welcome to keep working on the website and other technical aspects if you want."

The paper rattled as Mark folded it and placed it on the wicker side table. "No need to mention you're no good at that type of thing."

"You aren't, either," Donna pointed out. Her detective husband had grumbled on more than one occasion about the hardship of logging all his official activities onto the computer. On the other hand, he'd rejoiced in how easily he'd found files on his laptop from the comfort of his own home.

"I know," he grinned, not the least bit upset at having his lack of computer skills pointed out. "I'm grateful for Maria's technical know-how. For now, I'm off to use my much-vaunted police skills over at the regatta."

Having scooped up all the errant beads, Donna stood pocketing the items into her colorful happy dogs dancing apron. "Are you going to catch a murderer?"

"Bite your tongue." He stepped closer and kissed her cheek. "I'll give the con men who floated in with the regatta the eye to let them know they're being watched. I may have to remind the uniformed officers to pay attention to the crowds, not the boats or the hot lifeguards." He exhaled audibly. "Sounds like a full day's work to me, especially walking around in a suit jacket in the noonday sun."

It wasn't the first time her honey had complained about walking around in the heat. She patted his arm. "I'm not sure why you can't opt for something a little lighter. The bicycle cops get to wear shorts."

"Dignity. I need my suit jacket because it's a symbol of authority. It gives people confidence. I can't go running around in a flowered shirt and shorts like all the other yahoos."

"I suppose." Donna pursed her lips, not totally convinced the man couldn't get by with just a shirt and khakis. "What about wearing your badge on a lanyard like they do on television?"

"That's television. Besides, I don't want to announce I'm the law until I need to."

"Yeah, as the only person there wearing a sports jacket, you'll blend in all right."

Instead of replying to her sarcasm, he removed his pen and pad from his jacket, then removed the much talked about article of clothing. "Better?"

Donna made a slow circle around her husband, giving him a thorough inspection. "Much. I doubt your co-workers will recognize you without the jacket."

"Ha!" Mark forced a laugh.

Maria squatted to put down the squirming baby, who immediately crawled toward the red geraniums. A quick sidestep had Donna guarding the colorful blooms.

"How about the tie?" Donna asked, knowing she was pushing her husband's personal dress code.

"What about it? You bought it. It's a good one. A little more colorful than I might have chosen, though. What's wrong with it?"

"Do you need it? You'll look like a bank president who wandered onto the beach by mistake. You still have that air of one who doesn't belong there."

He grunted as he shoved his pad and pen into his pants pocket. "You'll have me rolling up my pants and taking off my shoes and socks next."

The comment had Donna glancing at his feet, which caused Mark to hold up his hand, which was either telling her goodbye or halting any more effort to change his appearance. He smirked and dropped his hand before trotting down the sidewalk, heading toward the beach path.

Maria asked. "You think he'll take off his tie before he hits the beach?"

"He will and will probably put it back on before he comes home, too." The thought made her chuckle and shake her head. "If he removed it here, it would probably seem like I was asserting undue influence. It's a control thing."

"I understand. Good thing you don't have any control issues."

"Exactly." Donna pointed to Baby Cici, who was trying to reach between her legs to grab a blossom. "You might want to take her to the back yard where there are fewer plants to be plucked."

Maria lifted her baby, holding her high and letting her chubby little legs dangle as she made faces at the darling. "My goodness you've changed, Donna. Before, you might have suggested a nap, playpen, or time to go home when a toddler caused this much trouble."

"True." She pressed her hand against her chest as the fact sunk in. "Those were other people's children. Not my own blood. They weren't nearly as cute and smart as Cici." She reflected for a moment. "I think we've all changed. Would you have ever seen Mark working without his jacket before?"

The suggestion made them both laugh. A low automotive hum sounded as a car pulled into the inn driveway interrupted their amusement and caused Donna to check her watch. "It's my candidate, and she's prompt. An excellent sign. I have a good feeling about this."

Chapter Two

D ONNA MENTALLY CONGRATULATED herself for placing an ad in the newspaper for Tennyson's potential replacement. Even better, she did it before the regatta. Wonder of wonders, someone actually replied. A woman named Rosemarie was coming for an interview. That was probably who just pulled in. Just maybe she would fit the bill, and Donna would hire her. Who was she kidding? The inn would be full of guests by the end of the day.

Guests would be demanding everything from extra pillows to crushed ice for the beverages they sneaked into their rooms. A few would insist on a better view since the website mentioned an ocean view with an asterisk. No one bothered to look below to read what the asterisk meant. If they had taken the time to read the small print, they'd know only certain rooms had ocean views and only in the winter months. To get a glimpse of the wind-tossed winter beach, it also involved either pushing your face up against the window glass or sticking your head out the window, not always a great idea in the winter.

Part of her wanted to remove the description, feeling like it went awry of the truth in advertising law. Of course, if businesses actually adhered to that, there wouldn't be fit, beautiful people in all the commercials for fast food or beer. Maria was quick to point out almost every Legacy accommodation listed itself as oceanside or ocean view, no matter where they were located in the town. At most, it was only a mile to the beach, which a few would walk while others bicycled. Maybe she should consider getting bikes for the guests.

A car door slam drew her eyes to the parking lot. A middle-aged woman sporting short ash blonde hair stood by her car. While the woman was unaware of her, Donna took the time to evaluate her conservative, coordinated, pastel pants suit. It suited her skin tone.

As if feeling the inspection, she turned and waved. "Are you Donna Tollhouse Taber?"

The woman had done some background work or gossiped a little with the locals and knew Donna had married Mark Taber. On the website, the proprietor was listed as plain old Donna Tollhouse. With so much as he did around the place, it only seemed fair to add Mark's name online. She should ask Maria to work his detective title into the site to keep any possible felonious guests at bay. With the number of murderers who had either booked or visited the inn, it felt like the smart thing to do.

"In the flesh," she shouted, then strolled a little closer not wanting the conversation to be open to anyone out for a walk. As she neared the woman, Donna remarked, "I take it you're Rosemarie? You called about the position?"

"I did." She bobbed her head in affirmation. "I'm excited about the opportunity. A bed and breakfast sounds like a lot of fun."

A good attitude. That was one box checked. Donna felt like she needed someone with a little extra chirpiness since she was low in that department. Obviously, the woman had no clue about working at a bed and breakfast, which could be a big negative. Most women who were Rosemarie's age had done laundry, changed sheets, and set a table numerous times. She had all the skills needed.

"It's fun for the guests, but a lot of work for the staff."

Noticing that the woman's smile wobbled a little, Donna hurriedly added, "There are good moments, too. Like when people tell you what a great time they had. Or even better, they go ahead and book for next year. A few even leave a glowing review. That's the best. It makes me happy to see folks enjoy what I cooked, too."

No need to add that some of her happiest moments were when a murder didn't occur at the inn, nor was the murderer a guest. She'd also not mention The Painted Lady Inn had somehow got a brief notation in a scurrilous book about haunted places. If it *was* haunted, she'd have noticed it by now.

"That's sweet."

Sweet. A word not very often associated with Donna. Best to get the interview over and start Rosemarie working. Maybe the woman could start today. There were plenty of aprons in the kitchen to protect Rosemarie's outfit. She gestured to the front porch where Maria and Cici were still standing. "Let's go in the front door. It allows you to get the full effect of how a guest might see the inn."

The two of them were approaching the steps when in the distance an odd siren sounded. The *woo wee, woo wee* sound made Donna sigh and look at her watch. Mark hadn't even been gone ten minutes and already something had happened. There was a distinct possibility he might not even be at the beach yet if he'd stopped to chat with the locals as usual. Dog walkers, fitness enthusiasts, and just plain strollers noticed a great deal of things and at times could help pinpoint the time of a crime or even finger a killer. Even though Mark would never call them informants to their faces, they were, to a certain extent.

The odd siren was the local police boat the city had picked up at auction. They must have assumed it was a boat built in the United States. As if the word *Polizia* didn't tell the tale. No one had thought to try out the siren before bidding on it. On the plus side, it certainly got attention, but not always the kind the police needed, such as getting other watercrafts out of the way.

Her first instinct was to text Mark, but as a business owner conducting an interview, she couldn't. Maria gave a slight nod as if understanding her dilemma. Thank goodness Donna's brother had the good sense to marry a smart woman as opposed to any of those empty-headed bimbos he used to date.

Donna gestured to her sister-in-law and child. "Rosemarie, this is Maria, my sister-in-law and her adorable baby, Cici."

"Hello," Rosemarie responded and stepped closer to cluck over the baby.

Typical, Donna observed with a smirk. Women of a certain age tended to react that way around babies. It might be a plus for the inn since couples often showed up with toddlers and on occasion, infants. Of course, Rosemarie had no way of knowing the importance of her sister-in-law to the inn's operations unless she explained it. "Maria is our webmaster. She keeps the website current and handles reservations. She also takes photos of the property for the brochure. On occasion, she helps out in the dining room. I guess you can call the inn a real family business."

"How perfect." Rosemarie gave a little sniff as if trying to hold back tears. "It must be nice."

Somehow, her cheery candidate had deflated a little in the last five seconds. As far as Donna knew, she hadn't done a thing to cause it. Her eyes met Maria's, who shrugged her shoulders and asked, "Are you okay, Rosemarie?"

The woman waved the question away. "Sorry. Didn't mean to get all melancholy. It's just the mention of family. I guess you should know I answered your ad because I felt like I needed a change after my father died. I've spent the last five years of my life nursing him.

Then, when he died, everything exploded."

Since Donna was not only an amateur sleuth but also a hardcore crime drama fan, she assumed the worst. "Your father exploded?"

"Goodness, no." She shook her head. "My family, as I knew it." She held up her fists, then forced her fingers open, then shook her hands to demonstrate. "My siblings expected all the assets to be shared equally. Demands about remembered items were made. It usually started with someone saying that he or she had been told a specific item was meant for them. Since I had lived in our childhood home for the last five years, there were immediate suspicions about missing items." She shrugged her shoulders. "I never inventoried anything. Anyhow, I'm without a home, and the part of the ad that mentioned room and board appealed to me most." She pressed her lips together, appearing pained. "I hope I didn't ruin the interview by spilling all my dirty laundry. It was just the mention of a family business, and you two seem to get along so well."

Maria handed the baby to Donna and gave the anxious candidate a hug while murmuring, "No worries. I'm sure Donna will hire you and give you a place to stay. She's an excellent cook so the board part is a real treat."

Even though Donna had pretty much decided to hire the woman because of her immediate need for help, she didn't like her sister-in-law making promises for her. On one hand, the woman had no choice but to work for her since she needed a safe place to land. "Let me finish showing Rosemarie the inn."

Maria released the woman and extended her thumb and forefinger to her ear, pantomiming she'd call Mark. Then, she scooped Cici from Donna's arms. More likely Maria would text, but they hadn't worked out a signal for that yet. Thank goodness for her sister-in-law and with a little luck, she'd have Rosemarie doing laundry before lunchtime.

The light streamed through the parted curtains, picking out reds and blues in the oriental rugs and adding sheen to the just polished wooden surfaces. Right before guests descended upon them, the inn always looked its best, which caused Donna to stand a little straighter as she escorted Rosemarie around. "This is our first parlor. Usually we use it for quiet activities such as reading. In the winter, I host a Victorian Christmas tea here."

Rosemarie pressed her hands together. "It sounds like one of those holiday movies. The good ones where the entire family gets together, and everyone gets along." Her voice wobbled on the last three words, but she managed not to break into tears.

"Moving on," Donna inserted, knowing she'd be no good at handling a tearful applicant. Even worse, no one on vacation wanted to be treated to waterworks. Somehow, she had to get the woman to buck up, or she'd be working short-staffed this weekend. The problem was she didn't know what to say. Sympathy wasn't her forte—action was. "The next room is what I like to call the entertainment parlor. Each room has its own television. Sometimes other guests, mainly men, like to bond over watching sports."

They entered a room with a huge six-foot television screen as a focal item with comfy couches and chairs clustered about. No need to mention when the guests weren't using the room that Donna enjoyed watching her crime dramas on the oversized television. It made her feel like she was a part of the crime-solving team.

"I see," Rosemarie offered without a waver in her tone. She pointed to a bookcase filled with board games. "I didn't know people played board games anymore."

"You'd be surprised. It is usually the millennials who use them the most."

THE BELL ON the front door jingled as it opened, forcing Donna to turn, expecting her sister-in-law and child. Instead unfamiliar children flowed into the inn as if water. Two headed for the first parlor, another one the kitchen, and the fourth shot by her and hit the stairs at a run. What in Sam Houston was going on?

A red-faced woman darted after them calling names. "Samantha, Jason, Tori, Alexander, come here right this minute."

No response to the shouted command. Donna bit her lip. Thank goodness no guests had checked in yet. The unknown woman was obviously the keeper of the ankle biters, but a sheepdog might be needed to round them up. Maybe her aging puggle, Jasper, might be up for the task. She whistled for her canine at the same time Maria slipped through the open front door with Cici. At Donna's pointed look, her sister-in-law mouthed the word, *Sorry*.

A clatter, then a thud came from the kitchen. Donna squeezed her eyes shut as she whispered. "Please don't let it be mother's expensive cappuccino machine."

Even though it had been a gift for Donna, her mother used it much more than anyone else, which was probably the reason Cecilia gave it to her. It guaranteed she'd get a decent cappuccino with every visit.

The orchestrator of this junior wrecking team addressed Rosemarie. "Are you the lady sleuth who owns the inn? The lady with the baby told me she was inside."

Maria. That's who she had to blame. There was an ominous *oops* from the front parlor, followed by the tinkling of glass breaking. "Good gracious! Round those children up before they burn the place down."

Jasper, who must have been napping in the dining room, cautiously peered around the corner, not certain if it was safe to come out. The appearance of the indulged canine caused both Rosemarie and the not so successful keeper of the children to fuss over the dog.

"Oh, what a darling dog."

"Reminds me of my Marvin."

The kitchen door swung open, exposing a towheaded, gap-toothed youngster. "Dog?"

"Oh yes," Rosemarie enthused. "Come see. I think he may be the best dog in the entire world. Wouldn't be surprised if he could do a ton of tricks."

Donna could have kissed Rosemarie because her words, no matter how little they were based on fact, had the desired effect. The glass breaker emerged from the front parlor wearing a unicorn shirt and a guilty expression followed by a smaller version of herself. There was the tap-tap of footsteps as the sprinter came down the stairs slowly.

Jasper squirmed with delight as several small hands patted him and queried Rosemarie about his tricks. It gave Donna a chance to address the woman who mistakenly thought her applicant was her. Hadn't she helped Mark solve ten murders? But she still couldn't be identified on sight.

"I'm Donna Tollhouse Taber, the sleuth you were looking for. How can I help you?" Her fisted hands found their way to her hips as she decided that she wasn't giving up Jasper just to help the woman with crowd control.

"Oh." The woman stood and held her hand out to Donna. "I'm Thelma, and I need your help."

Donna took the offered hand and shook it. The woman better not ask for babysitting services because that wasn't going to happen. "What do you need?"

The words sounded a little terse, but there was no way she wanted to keep the little rascals in her formerly clean inn. She and Rosemarie would have their work cut out for them to get the place up to snuff before the first guest arrived. Unfortunately, she didn't have the guest doors locked since she had been cleaning and had no clue what disaster awaited her upstairs.

"There's been a murder! I came straight here when I intuited it."

Intuited it. Maybe Donna heard wrong. "If you witnessed a murder, then you'd be better off calling the police. Don't you have a phone? If not," she pointed to the hall phone, "you're welcome to use mine."

"No." Thelma shook her head. "It's not like that. I didn't witness the murder. I felt it. There was a disturbance in the atmosphere."

This had to be a joke. Her brother, Daniel, always enjoyed a laugh at her expense. "Did my brother pay you to come here and say this?"

"No. Absolutely not." The hectic color in her cheeks had faded, making her pale and tired looking. She blew out a long breath. "I know things. Kinda psychic."

Police sometimes did call in psychics to find missing children or even bodies. Maybe the woman did have some skill. Didn't she just hear the police boat before walking in? "Did you see who was murdered and the murderer?"

"No." Thelma's brows knitted together as she wrung her hands. "The thing is, I'm just learning to be psychic. Don't really see things. It's just a twinge."

"Kinda like rheumatism?" Donna inquired, not feeling too confident that another murder had occurred in Legacy.

Thelma's eyebrows shot up. "What does rheumatism have to do with murder?"

It had nothing to do with murder, which was about the same as

Thelma's alleged psychic skills. There was a stir as one of the children stood up, tired of petting a dog who did no more than groan with doggy delight. Oh, this wasn't good. "Everybody outside, now!"

Donna shooed the entire group to the porch. Not sure how to get rid of them, she turned to Thelma and said, "I'll get right on the murder and promise to keep you informed of the details."

"Oh, thank you. I knew I could depend on you." She grabbed Donna's hand again and pumped it. "Never paid any attention to those who said you never did any of the detective work, and that you were just a publicity hound who rode your husband's coattails to glory."

Publicity hound. The words stunned her. Even though she wanted to ask who said that, she didn't. She had a twitch, a knowing, a feeling that she knew who would say such a dastardly thing, and she wasn't even psychic. Heloise.

Chapter Three

DONNA STOOD ON the porch, keeping her gaze on the faded minivan Thelma and her herd had clambered into. Flanked by Rosemarie and Maria, the innkeeper kept vigil, making certain she wouldn't be surprised by the thundering herd again. Normally, she didn't lock the inn doors during business hours. It wasn't exactly welcoming, but she might have to make exceptions. The van coughed to life, jerking as it pulled away. It appeared as if one little girl was waving. Donna smiled, thinking maybe she had overreacted to the children. Her hand went up to return the gesture when she realized the child wasn't using all her fingers. *Figures.* Her hand dropped to her side.

Rosemarie gestured to where the van had been. "Is it always like that?"

Before Donna could assure her would-be helper that nothing had ever happened like that, her sister-in-law fielded the inquiry. "Not exactly like that, but something similar. It happens now and then."

Donna shot Maria the stink eye, which she missed. She was too busy making faces at her progeny. Might as well accept the fact she was back to working on her own, get inside, and clean up the mess. It was only fitting that Maria helped. Then again, with the broken glass and who knows what else she might find, it would be better if her niece were safe at home. "Well, I guess you'd better head out."

She directed the words to her sister-in-law.

"Momma's darling is getting sleepy, which makes her grumpy. When Cici is unhappy, everyone suffers."

Since her niece had been named after her grandmother, Donna couldn't resist a poke. "The same with her namesake."

Donna shared a laugh with her relative, then waved her on her way. She turned to Rosemarie, ready to do the same without joking about her own mother in the process. "I guess you'll be heading out, too."

"Why?" Rosemarie blinked a couple of times. "Did I do something wrong?

Seriously? Did the woman actually think that Donna was rejecting her? Any sane person would be hot-footing it to their vehicle, but then again, Rosemarie had few options. "I thought after that highly *unusual* display," she made sure to stress the word, "you might forgo the job."

"Nope. The few minutes here have been a lot livelier than my entire life. I've spent the last five years driving my father to doctor's appointments, parceling out medicine, and watching more daytime television than I care to admit. In between, I called my siblings and informed them on more than one occasion that this might be it, in an effort to get them to visit Dad. Every day was pretty much like the next one. Monotony. I'd welcome a stranger blowing in with premonitions. Do you think there really was a murder?"

"No, of course not," Donna answered, equally stunned that Rosemarie was still wanting the job and by the fact Maria made no mention of what she had found out from Mark. It could be nothing that had anything to do with a murder or for Rosemarie to even think that.

A squad car shot by the house and swerved toward the beach,

canceling out the possibility that something hadn't happened. Something most certainly was currently happening, and she'd have to wait to find out about it like ninety-nine percent of the population. The possibility burned her biscuits. What was the purpose of being married to a detective if she didn't get insider information?

"Oh," Rosemarie said, sounding the tiniest bit disappointed. "I think we should go and clean up the mess inside."

"You're right about that."

They turned in tandem and entered the inn. Donna couldn't remember hiring her, but she wasn't opposed to the idea, either. However, she should really check references and such.

"Where's the broom and dustpan?" her new hire inquired with a lifted brow.

"I'll show you. Each floor has a utility closet where cleaning supplies, a sweeper, and linens are kept. It saves on dragging stuff around. We have a modest elevator, but even using it to tote stuff around is a hassle. This floor's closet is in the kitchen."

Donna pushed the interior kitchen door wide only to discover what the mysterious thud had been. The expensive coffee beans she'd purchased for the weekend set, who tended to be high in the instep, were scattered across the floor, along with the metal coffee crock. "Crapola!"

That was about fifty dollars of beans decorating her floor. Thank goodness the little inn wreckers had left already. She wasn't sure what she'd do if they were still there. She didn't want to find out, either. Most likely, she'd say something she'd regret, and it would be spread all over town, making her into a combination of Scrooge and the Grinch before they reformed their curmudgeonly ways.

"Woo wee," Rosemarie commented. "I'll get right on it." She started opening doors in search of the elusive broom and dustpan.

"Found it," she chirped, brandishing the two items. "Now all I need is for you to point me in the way of the trash can."

"Not quite." Donna put her hands on her hips and shook her head. "I paid a lot for those coffee beans. Had to special order them. I'll never get any more in time."

Rosemarie shot a doubtful eye at Donna, then glanced down at the coffee beans. "I know good and well there are all kinds of coffee down at the Piggly Wiggly. Some of it is expensive, too. Why in the world would you go and order coffee?"

It was a good question. Donna glanced around as if she expected someone else to be listening in to their conversation. Still, to be safe, she moved closer to her helper. "It's the regatta. We got all those fancy folks from New England staying here."

"Ahh," Rosemarie stretched out the word. "I see. *Yankees.*"

"That's right." Donna agreed, glad her new hire understood the gravity of the situation.

Instead of replying, Rosemarie started sweeping. When she had a dustpan full of beans, Donna pulled out an ice bucket for their deposit. Her actions caused her helper to roll her eyes.

"Oh my!" Rosemarie exclaimed. "I know lots of folks still have hard feelings about the war of Northern Aggression but serving dirty coffee beans is going a bit too far. It's right up there with spitting on someone's food."

"I'm not spitting on the food or serving dirty beans. I'll wash them, then dry them in the oven on low heat. That way they'll be double roasted. People pay even more for double roasted coffee beans. I won't charge them for that extra perk, though."

Rosemarie swept up some more beans and swept them in the pan. "If you say so."

Disbelief sounded in her voice, forcing Donna to go into more detail. "The Swiss were the ones who came up with the concept of double roasting. Usually, it was done when they felt beans were under roasted, but they soon discovered it made coffee less acidy."

The sweeping stopped, and Rosemarie cocked her head. "I know you cook and all, but do you go into detail about every little thing you make?"

Had she done that? It hadn't been her intention. She wanted to make sure no rumors got started about dirty coffee beans at the inn. As far as going into detail, she could ask Mark, but being a smart man, he'd have a diplomatic answer. "I don't know. Does it bother you?"

"No, just curious. I might even learn something," she chuckled, as she dumped the last bit of beans into the ice bucket. "You do the roasting. I'll go check the front parlor to see what else needs sweeping up."

"Fair enough," Donna replied as she carried the bucket to the sink. It was great to have an employee she didn't have to manipulate into working. Things were really looking up. With Rosemarie in the parlor, it would give her time to call her hubby and get the low down. She waited until the door swung closed before tapping out Mark's cell phone number. Mark picked up immediately.

"I'm surprised it took you so long to call."

Donna sighed. "You have no idea what it's been like here. All I need to know is if there's been a murder."

Even though she didn't think one had happened, it would be good to be in the informational loop. Background noises filtered through the phone. A few shouts, laughter, and a shriek made it sound like a typical day on the beach.

"Sorry to disappoint you. No murderers today. We did have a boat capsize. They're still working to get it upright."

"That must have been the sirens." Donna sucked in her lips as she considered Thelma's prediction. Obviously, the woman really wasn't good at the psychic stuff at all. That meant Donna's crime intuition was still intact.

"Most likely. Some of the crew were hurt and taken away in ambulances. Nothing major. Right now, I'm trying to determine how many crew members were on the *Foam Empress*."

"What?"

"It's the name of the sailing yacht which was predicted to win the regatta. It had all the bells and whistles on it. Waves weren't even that rough. Maybe it turned too fast."

Unfortunately, Donna didn't know much about regattas. They appeared to be boat races. Sometimes, they could also be rowing races, usually between college teams. The type they had at Legacy was rich dudes who could commission the best sailing yachts and hire professional teams to crew them. The winner had bragging rights, which would serve them better than the pitiful monetary prize and trophy Legacy put up for the race. Publicity only sweetened the deal.

"What happened?" Already, Donna's mind whirled with the information that the expected winner foundered early in the race.

"Don't know. Right now, I'm trying to discover if everyone on the crew has been accounted for." A shout in the background sounded more like a policeman than an exuberant onlooker. "I've got to go. They found something."

Just like that, he hung up without saying what they'd found. Donna glared at the phone, and finally tucked it into her pocket. At least when he got home, he'd tell her all.

The doorbell jingled. *Please don't let it be Thelma returning with her brood.*

Chapter Four

THE FRONT DOORBELL jingle had Donna running for the kitchen pass-through door. She paused, debating what she should do. It would be too late to lock the door if it was Thelma. On the other side she heard women talking in cultured, clipped tones she'd assume were used on transatlantic voyages of the Queen Mary or at boarding schools. Since she didn't know any old-money folks, she didn't know for sure. It must be her guests, two hours early, and they would be expecting to go immediately to their rooms. The thought had her wincing with the knowledge she hadn't even inspected the upstairs after a pint-sized tornado had torn through it.

"Good grief. What's wrong with that poor dog?"

Jasper. They were talking about him. Her mind gave her numerous scenarios with none of them good. Why hadn't she checked on her canine after the incident happened? Instead, she was more worried about her inn. What type of dog owner was she? Guilt perched on her shoulders, but it had to make room for apprehension. What had happened to her beloved canine?

Donna straightened her shoulders and pushed through the door only to find Rosemarie gesturing to Jasper and chuckling as she spoke. "Oh, those children. One must have left their sucker behind. Jasper loves children. He can't resist them."

Her aging puggle was turning in circles, trying to reach a sticky sucker stuck to his back, just far enough up to make it an impossibility for the arthritic pooch to reach. He probably thought it was an unexpected treat. He tended to eat anything that hit the floor, which had resulted in more than one trip to the vet. As for children, Jasper liked some, but he always reserved the right to retreat when they got to be too much. Donna silently observed Rosemarie engage in small talk with the guests, managing to keep a pleasant demeanor as if she was enjoying the experience. Suspicion grew as the guests discussed their day with Rosemarie as if they had just found a new friend. Her new hire might be really enjoying herself. After all, she'd spent the last five years in relative seclusion.

A tall, middle-aged woman with a sunburnt complexion that announced she was no stranger to the outside elements nodded to Rosemarie. "Hope you don't mind us showing up early, but the first heat was a washout. *Foam Empress*, who was supposed to take the entire race, made an ignoble belly roll. The other craft automatically moved up to the next heat. Anybody could win at this point."

Her shorter, older companion, wearing a wide-brimmed hat, possibly to shield her pale complexion, held up one finger and added, "Anyone can win, except the *Foam Empress*. She's out for this regatta." She gave a derisive sniff before adding, "Serves J. D. Sizemore right. He's bragged to every reporter and unfortunate individual within earshot how his yacht was superior to all the others and a guaranteed winner."

"Never been raced before, either," commented the sunburnt one.

Donna was gathering more details from the chatty women than she had received from her husband. It was apparent by how the women were interacting with Rosemarie, that they thought her a guest or possibly the innkeeper. It was time to clear up matters. A quick downward glance reminded her she still had on her old jeans and a t-shirt from her cruise that read: *I love big boats. I cannot lie.*

Normally, she would have changed before the guests arrived at check-in time. Guests who showed up way too early got what they got.

The tall one turned to Rosemarie. "I'm Eugenia Heyer from Maine. You may have heard of my family: The Heyer Furniture family."

Yep, Donna had heard of them. She'd bought a Heyer entertainment stand that didn't hold up under the weight of a television. If she were Eugenia, she wouldn't be bragging about it.

Rosemarie bobbed her head and sent Donna a panicky glance. Now the perky banter had faded away, and the woman had no clue how to respond. Did she think it was so easy to be an innkeeper? This was her opening. Donna strolled forward with a smile and an outstretched hand. What was that dark spot on her hand? An age spot wouldn't show up overnight, would it? A quick closer glance confirmed it was a coffee bean. Horrified, Donna withdrew her hand and stuck it behind her back just as Eugenia put out her hand for a shake.

"My apologies. I forgot my hands were wet. I was washing..." She paused, knowing the truth would not serve her in this situation. "...up when I heard you come in."

Eugenia gave her a dubious stare. "You are?"

"Donna Tollhouse Taber, the owner of this inn and your host."

This information caused Eugenia to do a double take, glancing first at Rosemarie, then Donna. It was easy to understand her confusion, especially considering one of them was wearing her job interview suit while the other, Donna, was dressed for cleaning.

"Oh," Eugenia managed to give the word a hint of disbelief and condescension in one single syllable, which was an accomplishment in a strange way. "I assume Cynthia and I should be addressing you then. Today's race was a fail, and we'd like to retire to our rooms. Tea would be welcomed."

There were the makings for tea on each floor pantry, if tea bags and an electric kettle, along with individually wrapped cookies and snack-size bags of popcorn would suffice. Somehow, she had a feeling this wasn't the type of tea Eugenia wanted.

Donna hustled behind the tall table that served as her reception desk and booted up the tablet they used to register the guests. It took forever to come up while Donna held a forced smile. Then she had a better idea. "How was today's race?"

Even though Donna expected Eugenia to answer, Cynthia did instead. "What a waste. J.D. Sizemore's craft flipped after about twenty minutes in. Of course, we weren't at the start. All we really got to see was the boat go into a wicked lean, throwing some of the crew members into the water." She shook her head. "If we hadn't promised Cousin Oscar, we'd come down to cheer him on, I'd probably have headed back to the airport by now."

"Oh," Donna said, hearing a clue in the making. Even though the tablet was up, she decided to inquire more as she typed Eugenia's name into the registry. "Cousin Oscar has a boat in the race?"

"That's what I said. It's a racing yacht, not a boat. Boat sounds like a shabby dinghy or something."

"That's what I meant. Racing yacht."

Eugenia and Cynthia were sharing the third-floor suite. With younger women, she'd expect midnight whispered conversations. With older women sharing a room, it was usually a matter of finance. It wasn't unusual for the impoverished genteel to practice economics when away from home.

Their idea of cutting back might be to cut down to three servants as opposed to five or wearing a gala gown twice to different events as long as the same people weren't there. At least that's what British television shows had taught her. With any luck, her inn wrecker hadn't made it to the third floor. Donna removed the room key from the locked box where she kept it. She used to hang them on hooks, but after a true-crime show featured a murderer stealing the keys from a hook, she changed her policy. A determined killer could steal her locked box and pry it open, which would mean another storage method would be needed, such as wearing the keys around on a giant keyring similar to the school janitor.

"I have your key. Allow me to show you to your room." That way Donna would get first peek at the room to see if it had been tossed. If it had, she'd act upset. Might even mention having words with the maid, then give the ladies a gift card to one of the nearby restaurants she kept for emergencies. Usually, her emergencies consisted of the electricity going out, which had happened once.

"Your luggage?"

"It's in the car. The white one with the Connecticut plates." Eugenia offered the car keys to Donna and said, "Have your boy bring in all the bags."

If Tennyson were here, he'd take offence at being referred to as a boy. Rosemarie held out her hand for the car keys. How much could the women have? They were only staying for the weekend. Still, despite talk about going to the airport, they did mention the car having out-of-state plates. It was a good bet they drove. People who drive to places tend to pack more.

As she handed the keys over, she added in a low voice. "Go through the kitchen. There's a side door to the parking lot, and you'll find a luggage cart in the laundry room."

Rosemarie's brow puckered, and her mouth opened as if she were about to say something but closed it. She settled for a nod in acknowledgment and headed for the kitchen.

The matter settled, Donna turned to her guests. "I'll show you up. Would you prefer the stairs or the elevator?"

"The elevator," Cynthia volunteered and earned a censorious look from her companion.

"This way," Donna gestured to the end of the hall where she had installed a lift a little larger than a dumbwaiter to meet the needs of her elderly or infirm guests. It was little more than a metal basket that took up valuable floor space. Having no padded walls or ceiling, every groan and creak the mechanism made could be clearly heard. One guest joked that it sounded like it might shake itself to death.

The three of them entered the contraption with Eugenia giving it a disdainful glance and murmuring, "quaint."

Donna started the elevator, mentally calculating their combined weight and was satisfied they didn't exceed the elevator's limits. The elevator started with a hum and a jerk and slowly rose, passing the second floor where Donna noted open cabinets at the food pantry. Maybe her upstairs raider simply delved into the foodstuffs, which would explain the sucker. She stocked each area with gourmet suckers, discovering that both adults and children liked the exotic variety with everything from mango melon to lemon ginger, which was more of a favorite with the older set. She'd return down the stairs and set that to rights.

The elevator stopped and fortunately lined up with the floor this time, which meant there was no stepping up or stepping down.

As they exited, Eugenia glanced over at her companion and said, "I'm sure you'll consider the merit of the stairs in the future."

"Maybe…" Cynthia replied with a mulish expression that didn't offer a definitive answer.

Donna was betting on her using the elevator or at least using it when not in the company of Eugenia. The suite, as Maria liked to call the slightly larger room on the third floor, was immediately to her right after exiting the elevator. Maybe she could get the ladies interested in the pantry, especially if they were traveling on the cheap, while she surveyed the room to see if any damage had been done.

"Your suite consists of two bedrooms, a sitting room, and a bath. Let me show you the common parlor and kitchenette for each floor." She cringed when she realized she'd used the word *common*. Normally, it was an acceptable word, but she was sure Eugenia would insist there was nothing common about her family. Too late for her to substitute the word *community*, but that might be a fail, too. She'd have to keep moving before any objections could be raised.

"Here's your parlor. Many guests enjoy sitting here having a cup of coffee or a homemade cookie while reflecting on their day or discussing their future excursions." She gestured to the two loveseats and wicker chairs grouped around a low table. "The fridge is stocked with drinks." They had no clue she had only stocked those expensive Italian sodas and water in fancy bottles for this weekend. It was an extravagance, but she hoped to stave off any reviews that mentioned cheap snacks.

A basket of homemade cookies, individually wrapped, was on the table. Thankfully, they were undisturbed, which gave Donna hope for the suite. She pointed to the cookies. "I made those this morning. Coffee and tea fixings are in the cabinet. Why don't you two fix yourself a cup of tea?"

"A cookie sounds good," Cynthia responded as she dipped her hand into the basket.

Her friend's face colored up as if she were ready to say something or had the tendency to act like a cartoon thermometer.

Donna was ready to point out no other accommodations in Legacy or in the surrounding county would have offered free cookies when Eugenia complained about the lack of high tea, but instead, the woman said nothing. She picked up the electric kettle, filled it with water, and plugged it in. There might be hope for the woman if she would stoop to making her own tea.

"Cups are in the cabinet on the right," Donna volunteered while being secretly glad she insisted on china cups as opposed to using Styrofoam or paper cups. While she considered herself environmentally minded, the china cups were more about setting a mood. For this floor, she had ones with delicate bluebells painted on them, which she bought at an estate sale.

Before anything else could be said, Donna trotted off to check the room. Inside, both beds were still untouched. No indents on the down comforters or sticky handprints, which was a major relief. Fluffy towels hung side by side on the rack for which Donna was very grateful. It looked like this room had been spared. Still, she felt there was an air of disturbance about it. Good grief, she sounded like Thelma.

The groan of the elevator meant Rosemarie was coming up with the luggage. She might keep the women occupied as Donna made a thorough inspection. Pillows fluffed, Legacy brochures on the sitting room table, and the remote was by the television. The all-important remote wasn't aligned perfectly, which caused Donna to reach for it only to find it was stuck. Good gravy! What was wrong with it? Humidity could get bad in the summer, but she never had issues with remotes sticking to surfaces. A sharp tug released it and the wad of gum that adhered to the bottom.

"Gross!"

This wouldn't do. All the televisions were the same, which meant she could switch out a remote. Although, since all the rooms were full, everyone would need theirs. Donna didn't have time to deal with degumming the remote. She stuck it in her pocket, then ducked into the bathroom to wet a washcloth and scrub the sticky surfaces. When she popped out of the room, Rosemarie was talking to the guests. Standing beside the ladies was enough luggage for a month-long cruise with several formal nights.

Bless her. Rosemarie had only been here less than an hour, and Donna felt the woman already deserved a raise, especially considering all the luggage she had just hauled upstairs. While the women were chatting, Donna slipped into the next room and grabbed the remote and a clean washcloth, with a mental note to replace both.

Donna scurried back to the trio and announced, "Your suite is ready. Allow me to show you around. Rosemarie can follow with the luggage after you decide who gets which bedroom."

Cynthia must have heard something in Donna's voice because she arched an eyebrow, pursed her lips, and cut her eyes to Eugenia. Apparently, the woman already sensed she'd end up with the lesser bedroom. It had probably been that way for years.

ONCE THE GUESTS closed the door, Donna let out a sigh. Her day wasn't over, but rather just beginning. She added a washcloth to the room she raided and saw no obvious signs of trespassing. All the same, she'd have to trot her own remote upstairs and work on gum removal on the other. With any luck she'd get the gum off and have her personal remote returned to the bedroom. Her sweetie enjoyed a little television before bed to relax. It sounded like today he'd need it a trifle more than usual.

No time for the poky elevator, Donna raced down the stairs,

leaving her helper to take the luggage cart down via the elevator. This way, she could make a stop on the second floor, which held the most rooms and probably where the most damage was done.

The telltale jingle of the front door alerted Donna that even more early guests had arrived. Good heavens! What happened to showing up on time or being just a little late?

"Yoo-hoo!" a familiar voice called out. "Where's my favorite innkeeper? Some coffee and macadamia chocolate chip cookies sure would hit the spot right now."

Oh no, it couldn't be.

Chapter Five

A GRINNING ELDERLY man with a full head of silver hair stood just inside the inn doorway. His arm was draped around his female companion, who was also of the senior set. A full can of hairspray may have been used to lacquer the woman's elaborate blonde curls into place. Even the coastal winds hadn't put a dent in it. Unlike the man, who appeared smug and proud, the woman's eyes sparkled with possible interest and curiosity.

Donna trotted down the final stairs and dashed across the foyer. "Herman! I can't believe you're here."

"In person," Herman responded, then chuckled as if his remark had been humorous. It hadn't.

"I noticed." Donna dusted a kiss on his cheek when she drew close enough. "What brings you to our neck of the woods?" Even though she was pleased Herman stopped by, there were no more rooms at the inn. There might not be any left in Legacy with all the regatta guests.

He turned to his companion and lifted his eyebrows. "Should we tell her?"

"It's no secret, especially after we tie the knot. We have to tell people sometime, especially if we want a double room at the center. Still, it's up to you, sweetums."

"True enough." Herman beamed, then turned to address Donna. "Where are my manners? I forgot to introduce my sweetheart, Lola, the woman who makes each day worth living. Donna, Lola."

Tie the knot? Had Donna heard right? Her lips twisted to one side as she considered her ex-neighbor. As far as she knew, Herman had never married. He let it slip once that he had a girlfriend before he joined the army, but she hadn't waited around. Donna had typed the man as a long-time bachelor, but she should have suspected something like this might happen. He left Legacy to go to the center to be with his war buddies and other seniors. Once a single man reached the age of seventy, if he wasn't an ogre, he became the equivalent of caviar to the elderly widows and female seniors. It followed, if Lola won Herman's heart, she must be pretty special.

While not normally a hugger, Donna felt the occasion called for it and embraced Lola. "So glad to welcome you to the family." She felt the need to clarify. "I know Herman isn't a blood relative, but he has always felt like a part of our family."

Lola returned the embrace, enveloping Donna in a cloud of classic perfume. As she stepped back, she rubbed a hand over her face while realizing Herman had not answered her initial question of why they were here. "Glad to see you, Herman." She nodded in Lola's direction. "It was a pleasure meeting you, too."

"Ah," Herman started. "I can almost hear the wheels turning in your head. Right now, you're probably thinking, 'do they want me to put them up for the night?'"

Since the man was on target, Donna waved the remark away. "Don't be silly. Of course, I can't put you up. The inn is full." Afraid she might have ruined his plans, she inquired in a softer voice, "You weren't expecting a room, were you?"

Lola sucked in her lips as if she had a secret, she was determined to keep but was having a hard time doing it. Finally, she let her breath out with a big whoosh and pressed her manicured fingers together. "We're flying to Vegas today. We're going to the Graceland Wedding Chapel to get married." She gave a little yelp. "I can't believe it. My dream has always been to walk down the aisle by an Elvis impersonator singing *I Can't Help Falling in Love with You*."

Herman gave his fiancée an indulgent look, and turned to Donna. "Lola's from Vegas. In some ways, it'll be like going home for her. There's so much she wants to show me. There's a dancing water display, a volcano that erupts, and some place that's just like a circus. And," Herman waved his index finger as his eyes lit up, "there's even a wax museum where you can take your photo with celebrities such as the Queen or Ann-Margret."

He gave a wistful sigh. "They're wax, of course. Originally, we planned to drive across the country, an epic road trip."

Lola made a face when Herman mentioned the road trip, then waited for a lull to add, "That idea lasted about ten minutes. I explained to Herman that he'd be too tired to enjoy our wedding and our honeymoon. Epic road trips are for the very young. I want to board a jet, be waited upon by a cheerful flight attendant as opposed to making a survey of rest stops that aren't memorable."

The two seniors giggled, resembling infatuated teens more than seniors. It was nice to see them so happy. A thump and the slam of the side door had Donna holding up her hand. "I need to check on that."

With a little trepidation, she pushed the kitchen door open, not knowing what she'd find. Normally, her former helper, Tennyson, would be in the back area serving as her first line of security. That only worked when he was in his room, not on the phone, didn't have earbuds in, and wasn't watching television. Truthfully, it didn't work all that well.

That's the problem with leaving doors unlocked for the guests.

Despite the murders Donna helped solve, Legacy was a relatively safe place. In general, the killers were out-of-towners and on a rare occasion, a local with a grudge.

Still, if she had to have open doors, it was important the general public, guests, and possible would-be criminals knew she had her own personal law enforcement officer inside the house. As a watch dog, Jasper barked at leaves, while usually ignoring actual threats. His wagging tail and intent focus meant it was usually an individual he knew.

"Who's there?" Donna called out in her best *don't mess with me* voice. A clatter came from the far side of the kitchen where her oversized commercial fridge resided. Its door stood ajar, and the back of her husband filled the open space. He turned, clutching a food container and a jar of pickles.

"Woo! I earned your I Mean Business voice. Sorry if I surprised you. I swung by for a bite to eat because I won't be making it home for supper." He grimaced. "That means I won't be able to help you with your mixer, either. Maybe you can get your brother, Daniel, or your mother to help."

Her husband not making it home at a decent hour wasn't unexpected news. Whenever Legacy hosted an event, the police force put in major overtime. "Regatta crowd, I assume?"

"I wish." He carried his containers to the island that had kitchen stools clustered around it. "Got any coffee left?"

"No." She regarded her husband with an experienced eye. He was hiding something. Normally, he was fairly chatty about his day. He'd make a point of mentioning anything weird or odd. With all the strangers flocking to Legacy for the race, there had to be plenty of peculiar goings-on. If nothing else, he'd complain about the crazy out-of-state drivers. His tight-lipped answer made her suspicious.

Too bad he had such an idiot supervisor who had mentioned on more than one occasion how citizens could not help with cases. She was more than a citizen. Without her, many crimes would have gone unsolved or might not have been solved in as timely a fashion.

Once Donna had the coffee brewing, she brought out the chips her husband preferred. "Here." She placed the bag in front of her husband and took the container of leftover meatloaf to heat. When she had her back turned to him, she announced, "You might as well tell me, or I'll be weaseling information from other folks. It'll probably be wrong, and I'll go off half-cocked, possibly doing something dangerous or stupid."

A derisive snort erupted as Mark inserted his hand into the chip bag. "Normally, that shouldn't serve as a form of manipulation, but since I know you, it does. Looks like we have misplaced a few members of the *Foam Empress* crew. One of them happens to be an important billionaire, J. D. Sizemore."

"Murdered?"

"Stop that! Everything is not necessarily murder." Mark bit into a chip with a little more vigor than the snack required.

The interior door swung wide, and Herman stuck his head into the opening "I thought I heard Mark."

Mark blinked. "What?" He glanced at his wife for clarification.

She gestured to Herman and Lola, who was a step behind her sweetie. "They're on their way to Vegas to get hitched by an Elvis impersonator."

"No," Lola objected. "An Elvis impersonator walks me down the aisle. A regular minister marries us. We need to keep it legal." She winked at Donna and Mark.

The remark, or maybe the wink, surprised the good detective, who coughed so hard he had to grab on to the edge of the island to stay upright. When his coughing frenzy passed, he cleared his throat. "Maybe I should be drinking water instead of coffee. That salt air must be getting to me."

Without being asked, Donna filled up a glass from the tap and gave it to her husband. "Here."

There was a momentarily lull in conversation as Donna heated the meatloaf in the microwave and Mark drank. The vintage cat clock's tail swung back and forth as its eyes moved in unison. *Click.* The tail and eyes moved to the right. *Clack.* They swung back to the left. The fridge made a low hum, competing with the buzz of the microwave. Herman broke the wordless pause.

"You have a missing millionaire. Good thing Lola and I arrived when we did. We met solving cold cases at the center. We are four for four on the cases."

If the commissioner wasn't thrilled with Donna putting in her two cents, he'd be less thrilled to know a couple of out-of-town seniors chimed in on the current case. Donna decided to say nothing and let Mark handle it. She was curious if he'd give Herman and Lola the same excuses, he used on her.

Before Mark could tell the couple thanks, but no thanks, Lola patted Herman's arm. "Sweetie, remember we drove down to North Carolina to see your friends and because we could get a direct flight from Charleston. We need to get going in a little while."

"You're so right." Herman rubbed his hands together. "Alrighty, you need to be quick. Give me the situation and my bride and I will see if we can work out any obvious motivations or skullduggery."

Her fondness for Herman kept her from mentioning if something was obvious the police would already know it. The microwave beeped, letting her know the meatloaf was ready. Donna swung by the fridge for the barbeque sauce her husband liked to douse on the perfectly good meatloaf. At first, she was insulted when he did but eventually realized it was a habit. He had cut back on drenching everything in catsup, steak sauce, and barbeque, using much less. She bustled around the kitchen, keeping one ear open for what Mark might say.

"Well," her husband started. "This is police business, but it will hit the paper soon enough. The yachts are racing in heats. If we tried to race all the boats at once, it wouldn't be fair. One would have to deal with the rocks close to shore; the ones in the middle get the breaking waves, and the ones farther out might get smoother sailing but have a longer way to go to reach the finish line. The boats start at Anston, and the finish is at Legacy. In Anston, the race started with the *Foam Empress* and *Josie's Obsession*. The *Empress* took a decided jump. This was to be a sail only race. The crew on *Josie's Obsession* radioed they'd heard a boat motor as *Empress* passed them. I'd call it sour grapes, but there were some other sailors onshore who stated the craft moved too fast for the wind that we had."

Donna presented her husband with the meatloaf and barbecue sauce. "Thanks." He smiled at her and waggled his eyebrows.

The man used his shaggy eyebrows for conveying messages the way most people use words. While he may think he had several meanings to his eyebrow waggle, Donna always saw it as whatever was the most obvious at the moment. "I'll get the coffee only if you finish the story."

He held out one hand to Herman. "Take note. See what happens once you put a ring on your beloved's finger. They blackmail you with food and drink."

Another woman might take offense, but Donna knew her husband liked to joke around. Two could play that game. "I did that before we were married."

"True," Mark agreed. "I might as well finish because I don't want the two of you to miss your flight. Did you plan on leaving your car in the parking lot?"

"Yes," Herman nodded. "Right now, we don't know how long we will be staying. It could be a couple of days, maybe a week. Me and my girl are fancy-free. By the way..."

His voice trailed off, and he stared at the coffee cup Donna placed in front of Mark. It didn't take a mind reader to know Herman wouldn't mind some java and probably some nibbles to go with it. "I'll get you both some coffee. Might as well take a seat at the island."

Once the two were settled with coffee and a plateful of maca-roons, Mark continued his tale. "I hit the beach about the time the *Foam Empress* came around the bend. I don't consider myself a sailor, but it seemed to me the boat was moving erratically. The other racing yacht wasn't even close. I barely had my foot on the sand when a yell went up from the crowd. It was hard to see with hundreds of people blocking my view. I could see the top flag on the boat, and then it vanished."

He paused to take a bite of meatloaf while the three of them waited—the equivalent of suffering through a commercial to get back to the actual show. While the rest of them watched, Mark sipped his coffee.

Finally, Donna had enough. She could tell when he was stalling. "Finish it."

Mark smirked at her and enjoyed another bite of meatloaf. After he swallowed, he gestured with his empty fork. "Here I was behind everyone and not able to see a darn thing. I got out my badge and worked my way through the crowd. When I made it to the front, I saw the *Empress* leaning and the crew scrambling around on the deck trying to right it. A big wave hit the boat, sinking it even deeper into the water. Some of the crew was either thrown from the boat or jumped.

"Wet crew members swam toward shore. Most were embarrassed. One had a broken arm. It was pretty chaotic. Then the police boat came with that idiotic siren going." He looked down as if the thought was too much to bear. "Anyhow, we didn't know who was still on board. I managed to corner a crew member named Cameron, who was merely wet. He listed all the people on board. There were four left on board. The Coast Guard came and rescued two people from the *Empress*."

Donna had been following the story closely. "I thought there were four people left on board."

"Yep." Mark picked up his coffee cup and drank. When he put it down, he reached for a macaroon and bit into it. After what seemed to be a lengthy chew, he said, "This is where the trouble comes in. Sizemore wanted to be on his craft. It was rumored he wanted photos of him onboard, possibly showing that he was sailing it. The race was a chance to show off his latest creation in his specialized racing yacht line. If he won, there would be tons of orders."

They were obviously at the root of the problem. "Where is he?"

"Not sure," Mark answered. "Where the yacht capsized wasn't that far from shore. The Coast Guard immediately swung into action. Outside of a captain's hat washing ashore, there was no evidence of Sizemore." He shrugged. "Not sure how good Cameron's crew count was. He named one fellow who would have been on the yacht but was on the beach with a neck brace on instead. He'd injured himself hang gliding and a replacement had to be found. He's one of the people thought to be missing. Obviously, he was on the beach."

"Wow." Donna pursed her lips, then audibly sighed. "Anything could have happened to Sizemore. He could have drowned. He might not have been on the yacht. Maybe he was abducted by aliens."

"That's not any help," Mark grumbled. He took another sip of his coffee and smirked in her direction. "However, you do get points for not saying he was murdered."

It was hard not to go there, but so far there was no real evidence. Donna turned to the soon-to-be newlyweds. "What about you guys? Got anything?"

"Umm," Herman stalled and rubbed the back of his neck. "Nothing. I guess true love has clouded my crime-solving ability. What about you, sweetie?"

Lola tapped a manicured nail against the island's surface. "You mentioned something about a racing yacht line. There was also some speculation about the *Empress* cheating. I think you need to look at who would benefit from Sizemore losing."

Donna's mouth dropped open, and she placed her fisted hands on her hips. *Oh no she didn't.* Insightful comments were her territory. "You two better get a move on. Don't want to be late for your flight."

Her hasty reaction might earn some censure from her hubby, but he glanced at his watch instead. "Donna's right. You better get moving. Every small-time news service hack and local station, with a few not so local, will be heading here to report on the disappearance of the flamboyant billionaire. Better get out while you can."

Chapter Six

THE BRAKE LIGHTS on the oversized sedan lit up once before Herman guided the car out of the inn parking lot. Mark and Donna stood on the porch and waved as the vehicle turned onto the road. The sun shone brightly, forcing Donna to use her flattened hand as a sun shield. "I'm not sure how I feel about letting the two of them drive to the airport on their own."

"Seriously?" Her husband arched one eyebrow and gave her a slight nudge. "You do realize they drove across two states to get here. I'm betting they can make it to Charleston."

"I know." She gave a little sigh. It was hard to explain. Everything was changing. First, Daniel married Maria, for which she was thankful. Then, Herman moved. She married Mark, which was good, too, and Tennyson graduated and moved on to Charleston.

"Wait a minute!"

"A revelation about my missing tycoon?" There was a hopeful note in Mark's voice.

"No." It was unfortunate she hadn't come up with anything on that front, but she would as soon as she put her mind to it. She pivoted to face her husband, which wasn't as easy as one might think in athletic shoes. "Charleston. I thought it was odd they were flying out of Charleston. All that nonsense about getting a nonstop flight to Vegas. I'm fairly certain every airline has nonstop flights to Vegas. It would probably have been no problem to get one from Indianapolis."

Her husband chuckled, wrapped his arm around her shoulders and gave it a little squeeze. "It's obvious he wants to show off Lola. Imagine a lifelong bachelor who thought he'd never get married, and then he hooks a sweetheart like Lola."

"She does seem like a winner. Just enough feistiness to keep Herman on his toes. That wasn't my point. We may think Herman dropped by to see us, and he did, a little. I believe he's on his way to see Tennyson, and there's a convenient airport nearby."

"Hmm. Makes sense." Mark used his free hand to stroke the beginnings of a five o'clock shadow. "Here I thought they dropped by for our blessing."

Donna leaned back into her husband's half-embrace and stared up at him. "Would you have thrown me over if I hadn't met your family or co-workers' approval?"

"Well…" Mark started, but his eyes stared off into the distance.

Her question was meant more like a tease, not an actual inquiry. Hopefully, she'd get an answer. The gentle art of turning aside a hard question with flattery was not in the good detective's playbook. He was more of a *just the facts, ma'am* kind of guy.

"I wouldn't bother asking anyone else's opinion since no one knows you as well as I do."

"So true." Not bad, considering what he could have said, but he wasn't finished.

"As you know, I've spent most of my adult life in law enforcement. Usually, when I get a call, it's not because everyone is happy with their lives. I've seen a lot of people hurt the ones they professed to love. It may have made me a little shy about settling down. I didn't think there was anyone I could not only get along with but also look forward to seeing at the end of a hard day. That was until I met you. So no, I didn't ask anyone's opinion on marrying you, knowing that what we have together is incredibly rare."

"Aww." Donna brushed a tear from her cheek and pushed up on her toes to land an awkward kiss on her mate's face. "That was so sweet."

"Yes, that *was* pretty good," Mark agreed with a grin. "I surprise myself sometimes." He gave her an extra squeeze. "I need to be heading out to meet with the officials from the start of the races. Lots of photos were taken. We should be able to narrow down if Sizemore was even on the yacht at the start. We might be searching for a man who is tucked away in some luxury hotel room sipping champagne."

It could be a possibility, but not one she considered. "What about the other missing crew member? Didn't you tell me that some guy in a neck brace said they had to get a substitute?"

Her husband's arm slipped off her shoulder as he exhaled audibly. "That troubles me. No real name about who they picked at the last minute. Apparently, Sizemore didn't sail with a few extras. It could have been a ruse just to get on the ship to sabotage it."

The iconic light bulb flashed into existence over Donna's head as she said with certainty, "Kidnapping! Notice I didn't say *murder*."

"I'm thankful for that." Mark paced the long porch with his hands behind his back. He completed one length. As he came back toward Donna, he spoke. "If that's what it is, no one has taken responsibility. There have been no demands for money."

"Yet." Donna felt it was important to point out that fact. "They could be busy trying to move the big shot to a secure location. You'll get a call later."

Her husband narrowed his eyes. "You sound so certain. Did you pick up some information I don't know about?"

Donna shot her right hand through her hair, mussing it even more. "Depends. I had a stranger show up with her pint-sized wrecking crew. She told me she felt a disturbance in the air."

Her husband grimaced. "A disturbance in the air, huh?"

"It may have been atmosphere. I wasn't paying too much attention since the kids had split up and were off in various rooms, undoing all my hard work. In fact, I need to check with Rosemarie and see if she discovered any more damage."

"Rosemarie?" Mark repeated the name as a quizzical expression crossed his face.

Normally, Mark could lock onto a name and tell you quite a bit about the person, especially if they'd been arrested. Her hubby had a mind like a steel trap. At that moment, she could tell he was coming up with nothing, but she wouldn't admit it to him. "My new assistant. Remember? I put an ad in the paper."

On cue, the front door opened, and Rosemarie stepped out onto the porch. "There you are. I had a question about the second-floor pantry." The woman stopped and nodded in Mark's direction. "I didn't see you there. Sorry if I interrupted."

Mark smiled, then glanced at his wife. Donna, getting the clue, cleared her throat. "Ah, Rosemarie, this is my husband, Detective Mark Taber. He stopped by for lunch."

He put out his hand in greeting and asked, "I didn't catch your last name."

Of course, he hadn't caught the last name. Donna hadn't given it. She had talked to Rosemarie on the phone but hadn't had her fill out an application or checked her reference. However, she seriously doubted the woman had any current ones since she spent the last five years nursing her late father.

"Wagner," Rosemarie offered. "It's great meeting you."

"Likewise," Mark responded. "Work calls." He gave the women a salute and turned toward the parking lot.

It didn't take too many of her deductive skills to know Mark planned to put Rosemarie's name into the computer database to see if she had any priors. The fact he was using the car meant he wasn't heading to the beach, which begged the question where was he going. No matter what time he arrived home tonight, she'd ferret out the information. Donna turned to her assistant, who waited patiently. "Something about the pantry?"

"Yes," she nodded. "I assumed you stocked it up."

"I did." She hadn't had time to do more than glance at it since Herman and Lola had arrived about that time.

"I assume you took out the trash, too."

"Of course, I did." What could the woman be hinting at? She worked hard to run not only a clean inn but a classy one, too.

"That's what I thought." She gave a slight shrug. "I found some empty cookies wrappers and some empty Italian soda bottles in one of the rooms."

The little rug rat must have chugged them. He could have pocketed some of the cookies. She considered the issue for a moment, mentally tallying how much the visit from the not-so-helpful psychic had cost her. She hadn't toured all the rooms, but it was adding up.

"We have replacement cookies and sodas. In fact, you should take a lunch break. Let me see what I can find for you to eat. Do you have any food allergies?"

"Not really, but my grandmother used to make me cornmeal mush when I stayed at her house. Not a fan."

Donna didn't think anything named *mush* would be a hit with her guests. "No problem. Come into the kitchen and rest your bones for a while."

"Okay," Rosemarie reluctantly agreed. Her pace slowed as she followed Donna. The window panels in the front door reflected back her helper's hunched shoulders and downcast head. The one-time chipper woman suddenly resembled a whipped puppy dog or one that expected a beating. Not understanding the sudden change, Donna went to what she knew best outside of solving crimes—food.

In the kitchen, Donna's normal domain, she hustled around, putting together a small salad and a healthy portion of quiche. "Would you like coffee, water, or a soda?"

"Coffee would be fine," Rosemarie practically whispered the words.

Something wasn't right. If anyone should be upset about the mess the kids made it should be Donna. She wasn't sure what caused her formerly chipper helper to turn into a whispering, anxious Annie. "Spit it out. Tell me what's wrong."

Rosemarie glanced down at her hands, then up at Donna. Her eyes were glassy with unshed tears. "Your husband is going to investigate me, isn't he?"

"Not really. He'll run your name for priors. Have you ever been arrested?"

"No." She said the word softly and glanced away.

Even though Rosemarie didn't say "but", Donna still felt it. Using her much-vaunted observation skills, she noticed her assistant had pulled her arms and legs as close to her body as she could without falling off the kitchen stool. Usually, this reaction happened when someone was fearful. "What are you worried about?"

Rosemarie cut her eyes to Donna, and then went back to staring at the wall. "You've been so nice to me, and I really like it here. You'll ask me to leave once your husband calls and tells you it's suspected that I killed my father."

Chapter Seven

A LIGHT BREEZE teased the porch wind chimes and a dog barked in the distance. Donna stood speechless in the inn's kitchen, clutching a coffee carafe and staring at her newest and only employee. Did she hear her correctly? It sounded as if she said something about her killing her father. The soft-spoken woman in front of her bore no resemblance to a murderer. Still, if mysteries from across the pond taught her nothing, never underestimate little old ladies or folks acting on grudges decades old.

Outside of someone hopped up on drugs or a robbery gone wrong, people usually had motivations for killing someone. Donna took an impulsive step back. Technically, Rosemarie should be grateful. Hadn't she hired her? She also put the woman to work without a chance to change out of her good clothes, which was rather high-handed. Her eyes scanned for a blot or stain marring her clothing that might send the unassuming woman into a deadly rage.

Noticing her survey, Rosemarie spoke. "Aren't you going to ask me if it's true?"

Well, most folks would or at least the nosy ones would. Prison was full of people who swore they didn't commit the crime or didn't have evil intent, even if the end result was the person dying. "Ah yes. Is it true?"

"Of course not." She gave her head an emphatic shake, then sighed heavily. "That might not matter very much since my brother can be very persuasive. He's in sales."

While many salespeople tried to interest Donna in everything from cleaning services to insurance, very few had any luck. She prided herself on seeing through inflated prices, pyramid schemes, and shady individuals. If Rosemarie was indeed a deadly daughter, Donna might have to take a long look at her deductive skills. Her abilities were top notch. No *ding* sounded when she met Rosemarie. In retrospect, all the murderers she'd met had rubbed her the wrong way before she even knew about their felonious nature.

It was nothing so obvious, like a crow sitting on the person's shoulder calling out, "Guilty!" It was usually such a small thing that she didn't remark on it. Only in hindsight did she know she knew, which was no help in the beginning, but did give her a sense of peace at the end.

So far, Rosemarie hadn't given her any reason not to believe her. Donna motioned to the carafe. "Let's get some coffee in you. Everything seems bearable with a shot of java."

Donna poured the steaming liquid into one of the thick, white, stoneware cups she'd bought for the inn. Considering the possible content of what her new hire might reveal, she went back to the cabinet to get a cup for herself. She might need it.

After pouring herself a cup and settling down on a stool, Donna nodded at Rosemarie. "Tell me what you think I need to know."

Rosemarie played with the ring on her index finger, and then cleared her throat. "My brother Ian was always the golden child in my family. He was the hoped-for son. Everything seemed to come his way. It didn't hurt that he was handsome and had some surface charm."

Good gravy! The woman was giving her the long version. She didn't need to know the forty plus years of bullying or how the brother chased away her only true love. Donna lifted the cup to her lips, considering what she needed to hear. Mainly, *I didn't do it, and here's the reason why.*

Donna coughed and glanced up at the cat clock—ninety minutes before guests start pouring in if they held to the actual check-in time. After that, it would be another three hours before their weekend mixer, which she would have to host without Mark's help. If she expected any family help, she needed to get on the phone—now.

Getting caught up in the guests' stories, her mother often forgot to count how many glasses of wine they'd imbibed and tended to overserve. Donna wanted to keep it to a two-and-a-half glass limit. Things were lacking even more with non-drinkers. A few insisted on expensive still or sparkling water that Donna told them weren't available. They probably assumed she meant they weren't shipped to this backward county. What she really meant was she refused to cut into her slim profit by buying fancy sodas and water. This weekend was her only exception to the rule.

When Donna tuned back into the conversation, Rosemarie had reached her teen years.

"Ah…" Donna started. "Could you cut to the chase? Why would you be accused of murder?"

The interruption caused Rosemarie to stop and blink. "I'm sorry. I tend to blather on." She glanced down, picked up her fork, and took a few bites of her quiche. "This is really good. I detect a touch of nutmeg."

Just like that, the woman was off the subject. 'Yes, there's some nutmeg in it." A good cook never gave away her recipes. "Murder. You were going to explain why your brother is accusing you of murder."

"Oh, that." Rosemarie forked up a few more mouthfuls of quiche. "About five years ago, my father received a diagnosis of liver cancer. It was fairly advanced. The doctor didn't expect he would live out the year, but he still advised treatment."

"They usually do," Donna found herself adding. She gestured for her assistant, who was now sampling the salad, to continue.

"Oh, this is nice, too. Do you sprinkle lemon juice on your salad greens?" she asked with a fork loaded with crisp greens, a carrot curl, and a cherry tomato.

All the questions about food might be a stalling technique, actual curiosity, or the woman was out to start her own bed and breakfast. "Your father. He received his diagnosis, and you moved in with him immediately?"

"No, that's not how it happened. He called my sister, Ian, and myself to discuss the situation. My mother was gone, and there was no one to look after him. He suggested one of us should move in and take care of him until he was better. Because of something the doctor said, he assumed a round of radiation and chemo would cure him. I was kind of hoping this, too."

"So, what did you do?" Donna kept glancing at the clock, not sure how she could hurry the story along. If there was a doubt in her mind, she couldn't allow the woman to bunk in Tennyson's old room.

"I burned through all my vacation and sick days at work toting my father to various appointments."

"What about your brother?" Even though Donna didn't want to lengthen the story, the sibling did figure into it.

"Ian was busy with his job and his family." She shook her head. "He came by about a half-dozen times after I moved in with Dad."

"Didn't you say something about other siblings?" Donna inquired, thinking she had heard the mention of more than one.

"Yes. There's Katrinka, my sister. She's in Germany currently with her military spouse. Because of her location, she didn't visit at all. As the youngest, she tends to side with Ian. He's good at influencing people."

So far, all Donna knew was Rosemarie's father had cancer, asked for help, and Rosemarie appears to be the only child who answered the call. The woman appeared to have a good appetite, which meant she might be open to some self-indulgence of the cheesecake variety. Inside the fridge waited a caramel swirl cheesecake she made for Mark, but he wouldn't mind giving up a piece to hurry along a story.

Cake cut and plated, she pushed it closer to Rosemarie. "Here."

"What's this for?" Rosemarie inquired, her eyes reflecting both confusion and yearning.

Pretty much the response she was expecting. "It's a treat to soothe the hurt of being called a murderer by your brother. I expect your father lived longer due to your care."

"His regular doctor said as much. The oncologist was unwilling to admit the treatments just made him weaker. It may have slowed down the spread of cancer, but it also made him homebound. That's when I decided to quit work. I worked at a mail-order auction house as a manager. We were always in competition with another company. Before I quit, things were tough because it was apparent, we were losing. My team was cut until it was me and one other employee. No matter how long we worked, we couldn't get it done. While I did quit, it was also a relief to be shed of the job."

Rosemarie took a deep breath and said, "Long story short."

A quick turn had Donna facing the cabinets to quell a strong yen to say *too late for that*. Fortunately, Rosemarie wasn't deterred by the action and continued speaking.

"Ian tended to forget that my father was open to any one of us taking care of him. I understand my sister couldn't help out being halfway around the globe. Our family home is big enough that Ian and his family could have lived in it. My brother didn't even consider the idea. He called it asinine. After I moved in, Ian only showed up when I called to tell him father took a turn for the worse. Eventually, even those calls failed to bring Ian around. Ironically, my father still talked about his son in glowing terms. The day the will was read, I was as surprised as anyone that almost everything had been left to me. What was more surprising was how much money my father had made on the stock market."

If Rosemarie inherited most of everything, including the stocks, why was she here? "Excuse me." Donna turned back to face the island and put up a hand. "I don't mean to interrupt. I just need some clarification. If you pretty much inherited everything, why are you even looking for a job?"

"Legal fees. My brother has everything tied up in court. He first tried saying I used undue influence as far as the will went. I had no clue what the will said since my father never mentioned it. All he ever said was that he'd take care of me since I took care of him."

"Makes sense." Donna caught herself stroking her chin the way Mark did and immediately dropped her hand. She'd heard married people usually started to resemble each other. The last thing she needed was her husband's heavy beard. "Still nothing about suspicion of murder."

"Oh, that." She said it offhandedly as if she'd forgotten mentioning it in the first place. "Ian told the lawyer my father would have lived longer if I wasn't taking care of him. The implication was I had a fat inheritance and hurried him along his way."

That was what she'd been waiting for? Donna had cut into the caramel swirl cheesecake for that? What a let-down. All the same, it proved her skills were still working fine since she had sensed nothing sinister about the female, even though she was putting away the cheesecake as if she hadn't eaten for weeks.

Still, some reply to her comment would be expected. "Poppy-cock. No one is going to listen to your brother. Five years is longer than most live with such a diagnosis. I expect your care kept him going. Don't worry about it." Donna didn't intend to. It did mean when things fell in place for her assistant, she'd disappear. As of now, this not-so-murderous helper was all she had, and court cases like that could drag on for years. It would be best to settle the woman's misgivings before a guest riled her up with outrageous demands.

A flash of light and a car door slamming shut pulled Donna to the front window to investigate if another of her Northern guests had the effrontery to show up early. What she saw chilled her more than an inopportune guest. The not-so-helpful psychic was back. This time, Donna was determined to cut her off before she got inside.

Chapter Eight

DONNA HAD SIGHTED her personal nemesis of the day from her kitchen window. Not wanting a repeat of the thundering horde, she was ready to cut off the approach before they made it inside.

"Rosemarie! Lock the front door behind me and do not open it unless I give you the secret knock."

Halfway through the front door, Donna realized she didn't have a secret knock. "Three fast. Two long."

Before the deadbolt clicked shut, there was a murmured, "What…?" which didn't bode well for Donna. Still, she had keys. In response to that thought, she patted her hands down her jeans. No keys on her. They had to be in her purse, which was in the bedroom. Her lips pulled into a frown. On the bright side, if she couldn't get in, neither could the frantic woman dashing up the walk.

Where were the destroyers of peace and harmony? Not a sign, which meant they were probably surrounding the inn and trying all the entrances on the side and back. She turned slowly, scanning azalea bushes and large decorative pots filled with petunias and geraniums. No smirking ankle-biter stared back at her from the shadows of the majestic oaks. *Nothing.* Where could they be? Her heartbeat galloped when she realized the side door was unlocked since Mark had used it when he'd stopped by for lunch.

Donna started hammering on the front door, anxious to relay

the information about the unlocked side entrance. No reaction. Apparently, Rosemarie was waiting for the special knock. What had she said? Two long knocks, two short ones or was it four short ones and one long? For all she knew, the youngsters were already in the inn and had already tied up and subdued Rosemarie. She didn't strike Donna as someone who could outsmart the wily youngsters. Donna tried the first with no luck and was ready to try the next when a hand landed on her shoulder.

She jumped, and then swung around, ready to tell the psychic to take her predictions and leave and to make sure she took the children, too.

"Thank goodness you're here," the red-faced Thelma gasped. Up close, there was evidence of tear tracks. "I need your help!"

Normally, Donna was flattered when people asked for her assistance, but she might take a pass this time. "Where are your little darlings?"

"Their mother picked them up. I agreed to watch them while she went to the dentist. I don't think I can handle more than a few hours of those kids. I'm just glad she came because I knew if I showed up with them, you wouldn't let me in the front door."

"You thought right," Donna declared and placed her fisted hands on her hips as she surveyed the yard for a little head to pop up. She wasn't convinced the children weren't cleverly hidden, just waiting for an open door. They were tiny guerilla soldiers bent on consuming snacks and wrecking rooms. "Is there another disturbance in the universe?"

"Yes." A sob escaped. "It's my brother."

What was this, the day for brothers? Surely there couldn't be another nefarious sibling up to no good. Donna inhaled, knowing she wouldn't like whatever Thelma had to say, but the evidence of tears did penetrate the hard armor of practicality that she donned every day. "Is he keeping you from your inheritance?"

"No." Thelma blinked a few times and shook her head. "Mom is in Mexico living the life of an artist." She shrugged her shoulders. "Whatever that means. Dad married a younger woman and started on his second family. I'm fairly sure there will be no inheritance. If we had money, I wouldn't have rode herd on those children."

Donna murmured to herself. "Didn't ride them too well."

"What?"

Thelma had heard her. Some people had better hearing than Donna expected. "I said, what about your brother?"

If things weren't problematic enough, the neighborhood dog walkers with their oversized standard poodle picked that particular moment to slowly stroll by. In the process, they shot Donna a peculiar look. No doubt they saw her blocking the door to the inn, which wasn't the welcoming image she wanted. Despite her previous efforts to win over the neighbors, Donna hadn't accomplished it. Instead, they insisted the inn was bringing property values down in the neighborhood.

Donna managed a pleasant expression and gestured to a nearby chaise on the porch. "Why don't you sit down, and we'll talk about it."

The wicker chaise creaked as Thelma took a seat. Donna took the chair that was angled slightly toward her. The chairs were intentionally put in conversational groupings so people could chat as opposed to staring straight at the street. It was a genteel neighborhood, but the actions of her neighbors wouldn't entertain her guests.

"Ok now, tell me about your brother." Even though Donna wanted to add *in twenty words or less*, she didn't. It took a hard inhale not to.

"Look at you. You don't even know Jimmy Bobby, and you're already fixing to bellow at the horrible hand the fates have dealt him."

Did this woman not understand she wasn't the bellowing type, especially when the situation involved someone with two nicknames? It was hard to be upset about something she knew nothing about. "Your brother?" Donna prompted.

"Oh." Thelma pressed her hands together and pushed them to her heart. "He's in trouble." She shook her head and sighed. "It started when he agreed to go work on this fancy boat. It was a day job. Promised to pay him in cash, which was good. If the old guy won, Jimmy Bobby might get some more work out of it."

Donna felt a tingle at the back of her neck. Her deductive skills were working, thank goodness. She'd even bet she knew exactly which boat the brother was on. "Was he crewing on the *Foam Empress*?"

Thelma's nose wrinkled, and her brow furrowed as she considered the question. "That's a silly name for a boat. Usually, men name their crafts after girlfriends or wives. I doubt there's anyone out there named *Foam Empress*."

"True enough. You said he was working on a boat today?"

"Uh-huh. He works for a temp agency, and they call him when a position comes available that he might want."

"Has he ever crewed a sailing yacht?"

Thelma inhaled, then grimaced. "The only boat I know about is when he worked on a shrimper. Whatever it was, he felt he could do it. There aren't so many jobs out there that you can be picky about them. He took it, and now he's being questioned by the police."

Talk about an optimistic jump. A man was ill-qualified to crew on a sailing yacht and suddenly the police are questioning him. Something didn't add up. "Why are the police talking to him?"

"Turns out the big shot who owned the boat is missing. Jimmy Bobby was pushed overboard when the boat was in open water. He's convinced it was deliberate. Thankfully, he's a good swimmer and some folks out on a skiff fished him out."

Looks like she'd need to don her detective hat. Too bad her tablet and tape recorder were inside. "Did whoever fished him out see him get pushed off the boat?"

Her brows furrowed, and her lips pushed out as she considered the question. "I don't think so. There was time enough for my brother to see his life flash in front of his eyes since he was certain he'd die out there."

No need to mention the race hugged the coastline. Maybe the brother wasn't as good a swimmer as Thelma thought. Apparently, the psychic skills weren't kicking in, either. "What do the police want to know?"

"Why was he in the water? Why didn't he finish the race? Stuff like that. I need to drive up to Anston to check on him. I stopped by here because I have a feeling, I might need your detective services.

No one had ever hired Donna for investigations. She'd always did the work free of charge. It sounded like Thelma wouldn't be able to pay, either. If she did take the case, she might be working against her husband. There was a good chance that Jimmy Bobby was their prime suspect. Was he guilty or just an unlucky fellow in the wrong place at the wrong time?

Chapter Nine

DONNA RESTED BACK against the cushioned porch chair and watched Thelma drive off in a burst of oil-rich smoke. Nothing had been resolved as far as Jimmy Bobby. His sister expected her to clear the man of any unfounded charges. At the present time, Donna had no clue how innocent the brother might be. Maybe she could uncover information that might clear the brother or find evidence of guilt, which would prove to Mark's stubborn boss that citizens could be useful in investigations.

The sound of a door closing caused Donna to jerk upright. What now? Hopefully, not more early guests, but they'd show up in cars or at least a taxi. All the same, she had no time to sit around and speculate. In a burst of energy, Donna darted to the front door and knocked wildly. No response.

At least the side door was open. Donna jogged down the steps and was almost to the parking lot when she heard a car starting. *Oh no.* She burst into a full-out run just in time to see Rosemarie pull out of the lot. It had to be the shortest employment in the history of bed and breakfasts. The modest sedan stopped at the edge of the parking lot, and the passenger window went down.

"No worries, I locked the door behind me. I'll be back in a jiffy." The window went back up, and the car zipped away.

Great Scott! Had she possibly said *what else could happen*? She thought she hadn't, but who knows? So much had been happening in the last couple of hours. It made her former job as a nurse in post-surgery look easy. No keys and no chance her guests on the third floor would wander down and let her in. Her sister-in-law and her husband had extra keys, but it would take time for either one to get here, which she didn't have.

Donna marched around the house, glaring at each closed ground-level window. It would be easy enough to push in a screen. Whatever happened to people leaving windows open to feel the ocean breeze? Everyone had to have air conditioning. Without it, they'd write whiny reviews about squalor and feeling like they were in a Third World country inn. Never mind the same people would pay twice what she charged to stay in a tent on a platform, call it glamping, and think it was wonderful.

On her second time around, Donna realized this wasn't her first incident of being locked out. Tennyson locked himself out so much Donna created an extra set of keys and hid them on the property. Her lips lifted in a grin once she discovered an answer to her problem. She never told her husband about the extra keys since he would have told her how dangerous it was. The good detective would say something about them being murdered in their sleep.

This would depend on someone wanting to murder them and knowing where she hid the keys. Didn't she put them in the rock that had a hollowed-out place just for keys? She started toward the patio that had wrought iron tables and chairs for those who like their breakfast al fresco. Besides oversized urns filled with blooming flowers, there were a few decorative rocks arranged around them.

By the time the rock was found, Donna remembered she changed her mind about using it. Her mother had told a story about someone whose house was robbed by the person finding the house key in a similar rock. That had made her find a different place to hide. Something not so obvious, out of place, or wouldn't be easily noticed by someone up to no good. The knothole in the sweet gum tree was low enough for her to reach, but shouldn't attract attention. At last, her planning ahead stood her in good stead. She hurried to the tree and crammed her hand inside the hole. Her fingers came up against something furry. Not good.

She pulled her hand out in a hurry. It didn't stop a red squirrel from poking its head out of the hole and scolding Donna with high-pitched chatter. It looked like the hiding place was now the home to a family of squirrels. There was a good chance the squirrels had thrown out the key or it was in the basement of squirrel central.

No help for it. She was going to have to break into the inn. It would mean extra money spent to fix the side door, but she knew that was the easiest one to jimmy. A crowbar, a knife, or anything sharp and pointed should help her get the door open. Unfortunately, she didn't happen to have either. Her exacting standards didn't allow such helpful tools lying around. MacGyver, a hero from a long-ago show, could make do with found objects. Not much here, unless she could pick up one of those flowerpots and throw it through a window.

Not workable, but there was a metal grinning sun on a stick that just might have a sharp point. Donna plucked the sun from the pot and examined the pointed end. Good. Things were starting to go her way. An uneasy feeling settled around her shoulders. She couldn't say what it was. Probably had to do with breaking into her inn. However, it may have had more to do with her having to resort to such drastic actions.

Metal sun in hand, Donna ascended the few stairs that led to the side door. Even on a day where many things did go wrong, she still retained a little hope and tried the door before going to work on the lock. The knob didn't turn, but she could hear Jasper barking on the other side. The door never closed that well, which was why Mark checked it every night before retiring.

She gave it a little push, and it swung open. Mercy. She'd spent all this time trying to get into the house and never tried the door until now. At last she could get to work on everything she needed to do. In the distance, a siren sounded like it was headed to the beach.

The siren grew closer as Donna stepped into the back hallway. She'd made a note to ask her husband what had happened when he arrived home. Car tires crunched the gravel as the siren sound grew louder. Jasper joined in the cacophony.

One of Legacy's finest jumped out of the car. It was Officer Wells, the patrolman who bought Mark's house. She always liked him.

He dashed up the two stairs, leaving his car door open. "Donna, are you okay? We got a call that a breaking and entering was in progress."

"What is this nonsense!" She folded her arms and inhaled deeply. "I've walked around this inn several times in the last ten minutes. I think I would have noticed if someone was breaking in. Who in the world called you?"

Wells cleared his throat and glanced down at the floor before replying, "She said she was a guest. Is that possible?"

"Could be." Donna was putting her money on Eugenia as the culprit.

"Okay." Wells spoke into his shoulder-mounted radio. "False alarm. Make sure to notify Detective Tabor." He turned and smiled at Donna. "How did you get locked out?"

She was tempted to laugh and say it was a funny story, but she didn't feel like laughing. It wasn't funny, either. "My newest employee locked me out."

"Sounds peculiar to me. Maybe you might want to rethink your new hire." Wells shot her a sympathetic glance.

"Trust me. I am."

Chapter Ten

B Y SIX THAT evening all the guests had checked in. Donna had managed to convince her brother, Daniel, to help with the evening mixer. The radio played soft rock classics as she lined up the various trays for the appetizers. Afraid a guest might accuse her food of being ordinary and bland, she researched the net for new ideas and called in a couple of favorites from her friend and restaurant owner, Janice, who was good enough to send around some petit crab cakes with dipping sauce. If anyone praised them, Donna was supposed to direct them to the Croaking Frog for more. If they made the mistake of criticizing, her job was to deck them, not that she'd do such a thing. Her friend was probably joking, but Janice wasn't a fan of criticism.

Her cell burbled as she washed the bibb lettuce intended for the boiled shrimp platter garnish. Drying her hands, she murmured to herself and possibly Jasper, who was watching intently for any dropped goodies. "This better not be one of the guests calling to tell me he has a seafood allergy."

The reservation form very clearly stated that food restrictions needed to be mentioned at the time of booking. It amazed her how many people assumed she'd have almond milk, gluten-free bagels, and tofu tucked in her kitchen. She used to, but it all went bad waiting for someone to request it.

She wiped her hand on a towel and picked up her phone. Mark's number and smiling face flashed across the screen, which was a relief. "Hello, sweetie. What's up?"

"We have a person of interest."

"I know."

"You do," he joked. "Maybe you can tell me his name then."

"Jimmy Bobby." Her eyes rolled up as she tried to recall Thelma's last name, which might not be right since Thelma could have changed her name if she'd married.

"Son of a gun! What are you, psychic? Did Wells tell you when he went by?"

"No. The psychic, Thelma, came by again."

A snort sounded in Donna's ear before Mark started speaking again. "Here I thought I had a crazy day. Are you the one who called the police just to get rid of the children?"

She chuckled. "Legacy's Finest would have a full-time job rounding up these wayward children. No, that's the parents' job. One of our uppity guests called, certain a disreputable character such as myself was trying to break into her own inn."

"I'm so sorry. On the good side, at least it was Wells who showed up. You wouldn't want one of the new guys you've never met showing up and trying to haul you away in handcuffs. Maybe you need a uniform with the inn name on it. It might clear up some issues."

Didn't the man realize she had just stopped wearing the nurse's uniform she'd donned for the last thirty-plus years? "My sunny smile and welcoming manner are my uniform."

Instead of agreeing, her husband said, "Your psychic must be okay if she guessed the name of the suspect. Why did she come by that name anyhow?"

"Oh, the suspect is her brother. He called her from Anston. She assumed he was in trouble because he took a crewing job from a temp service that he was ill-qualified for and somehow ended up overboard. No worries, though. He's a good swimmer, or so the sister said. On the upside, she didn't bring the children, who weren't hers, the second time. She was only watching them, which could explain their behavior."

"Hmmm. Sounds like you know as much as I do. Maybe more. Most of what I got from Jimmy Bobby was he was afraid of dying, and the other crew members were not the least bit cordial."

"Sounds about the same. He told his sister he was pushed overboard."

"Yep. Same here. I had to let him go. Being a lousy sailor is not an arrestable offense. You never said why she came by."

"Oh, that." Donna wrinkled her nose, already picturing Mark's face when she told him. "She wanted me to use my deductive skills to prove Jimmy Bobby is innocent in the disappearance of J. D. Sizemore."

Mark grumbled something unintelligible that Donna wasn't certain she wanted to know. "I didn't tell her yes or no. She just told me the story, then headed off. No worries. I am much too busy to get involved."

The side entrance door slammed, causing Donna to direct her attention to the back hallway opening. She expected to see her brother. Instead, it was Rosemarie, pulling a suitcase and carrying an oversized duffle bag.

A derisive snort indicated how much her husband believed her non-involvement. They'd talk about it later.

Donna told him, "I have to go. Daniel has agreed to stand in for you as wine steward and bouncer."

"Good deal. He's taller, younger, and more muscular than me

from working construction. People will listen to him."

"You're right." It pained her to admit that the men would respond to her brother's authority more than her own, especially the belligerent ones. Thank goodness she had a brother who didn't mind pinch-hitting for Mark. "Love you, bye."

Mark mirrored her final words and hung up. The oven buzzer went off, forcing Donna to hold up one finger to her sometime helper. "Just a minute. I have to get the eggplant parmesan dip out of the oven before it dries up."

Donna moved the tiny cast iron skillets full of bubbling deliciousness into a long pan of hot water, which she covered to keep the dip warm as she prepared the rest of the appetizers. That done, she turned and faced Rosemarie, who looked a bit weary and woebegone. The luggage indicated the woman had no plans of leaving a position that promised a room.

"Why in the world did you head out of here like a cat with its tail on fire?"

She didn't mention the part about being locked out of her inn because she felt part of the blame was hers. It might be smart to get one of those keyless entry door locks. With no time to waste, Donna slid the desserts out of the fridge. On second thought, her helper should be helping.

"Drop your stuff, wash your hands, and start helping me plate this stuff. You can talk as you work."

Rosemarie quickly followed Donna's instructions. She showed a natural instinct for the arrangement of tiny eclairs, and cheesecake wedges using mint leaves and strawberries as garnish. "I'm so sorry to have left in a hurry the way I did. You may remember I told you I've been living with my father in our childhood home. Despite the fact the home went to me, my brother is disputing it. He apparently called a sheriff to have me thrown out. Not sure if I was going to be locked out or what, and I don't know the procedure, I ran over to get my stuff when Dad's neighbor called to tell me the sheriff was there."

"What did the sheriff say?" Donna asked. Her first instinct was to tell Rosemarie to stay in the house to keep possession. It sounded like the brother was showing his true colors. There was a good chance he'd change the locks the first time Rosemarie left if he had a housekey. He might even be doing it now.

"He was gone when I arrived, but I got my stuff and thanked my neighbor. I told her about this job, which she called a miracle just at the right time. I have to agree with her." Rosemarie managed a wobbly smile.

Mercy. There was no way she could let such a desperate soul go. At least she made up a nice serving platter. Donna hoped the mixer would go well. With any luck, she might pick up helpful clues from the guests.

Chapter Eleven

MELLOW JAZZ FILLED the inn dining room as guests milled about and chattered about the day. Even though it was seven at night, the fading rays of the sun still illuminated the outside. On the coast, instead of long, romantic sunsets, the golden orb just dropped out of view, leaving darkness in its wake. This could be an issue with those walking along the beach. Locals knew enough to bring flashlights, but tourists weren't that savvy.

The possibility made Donna smile, and not because she was a fan of the unwary stumbling around on a dark beach and falling into the surf. Instead, it made her think of her friend, Janice, who owned The Croaking Frog, a restaurant that fronted the beach. Her friend bragged that the well-lit restaurant would be a beacon in the dark that a tourist would naturally gravitate toward. Once near, they'd inhale the intoxicating smell of her award-winning clam chowder. Normally, Donna would have picked up some chowder, but New Englanders had their own version and might not look kindly on another. On the other hand, maybe they were tired of the tomato-y chowder.

Her brother's voice boomed across the room as he inquired if a person might like a refill on their wine. Since Daniel worked in construction for two-plus decades, his hearing wasn't what it could be. People tended to forgive his overloud speech since he was genial and good-looking.

His loudness made it hard to eavesdrop as she picked up used plates and tidied the server. All she'd heard so far was the race coordinators were smart enough to throw in another heat since the first one was a wipeout for the *Foam Empress*. It wasn't clear if the other yachts had been standing by to race or if it was a spur of the moment thing. It made her wonder if Eugenia's cousin was in that heat. If so, the ladies missed the whole reason they drove down to Legacy.

At least that was the reason they were giving for being there. It could be home wasn't as pleasant as they pretended. She might pick up useful information since Eugenia and Cynthia sat alone, not mingling with the other guests. Maybe they thought themselves superior to the rest. It didn't stop them from enjoying the free food, though. By Donna's count, Cynthia had enjoyed two full plates of yummies, while Eugenia packed away three. They were obviously making a meal of it and making Donna hoof it back to the kitchen for more food. It wouldn't be fair for the others to do without.

Still seething from having the police called on her for trying to get into her own inn, Donna didn't trust herself to address the women. Rosemarie went in her stead. Besides, they liked Rosemarie. Weren't employees supposed to assist their employers? The problem was Donna couldn't instruct her hire to get the women gossiping and squirrel away the information for later as she might with her mother or sister-in-law. It would be quite an investigative effort to retrieve the information from Rosemarie without her knowing.

A tinkling of glass hitting the hardwood floor made Donna cringe. There was a belated *oops*. Someone must have had too much to drink, which meant their lips would be extra loose. Donna galloped through the kitchen to get a broom and dustpan to clear away the glass.

When Donna returned, she found Rosemarie reassuring the clumsy female guest while she picked up the shards by hand and placed them into the bowl she'd made of her frilly apron. Daniel put down the wine bottle to help and used the linen towel that had draped his arm to dry the floor. Drat! She'd missed her opportunity.

The petite woman who had dropped the glass was laughing. Her laughter was a bit too loud and out of control. It made her wonder how much the woman had to drink. She could ask Daniel, but he wouldn't know if the woman had already had a few drinks before she even arrived. Guests weren't above bringing their own alcohol, either. Still, tipsy guests didn't mince words.

Donna placed the unneeded broom and dustpan in the hallway. A platter of sweet treats, including tiny lemon meringue tartlets and brownies, waited in the kitchen. Her intention had been to place them on the server after the savory snacks had been devoured. If she walked around with the platter as if part of the catering staff, not only would she hear more, but she'd also get a good idea which dessert the guests preferred.

Most of the desserts vanished on mixer nights, but she was curious which one went first. That would be the favorite. Donna dashed into the kitchen, hoisted the loaded platter with one hand and backed out the kitchen door hips first to protect her precious tray of sweets.

Just before she turned into the dining room, she pasted a smile on her face. Conversations spilled out from the parlors, demonstrating a few guests had drifted out of the dining room, perhaps seeking out a bit of privacy. She'd hit both parlors on her way back. Right now, she needed to know what Tipsy Laugher had to say.

Donna nodded at the various guests and brandished her tray. "Dessert anyone? Take two since they're small."

Easy to say since two would make an actual serving. A murmur passed through the crowd, and people were milling around her to grab some more calories. Not exactly the result Donna wanted, but she held steady under the onslaught. Why not? Early on in her nursing career, she handled the emergency room on more than one full moon weekend. That was nothing compared to this. All the hands, plus the bodies pressed around her sucking up the available air, were making Donna a trifle uncomfortable, making her wonder if she had a touch of claustrophobia. The people backed off once the desserts had vanished.

Tipsy Laugher hadn't been part of the feeding frenzy. Her perfectly painted mouth fell open in surprise as she examined the platter. "They're all gone!"

The irate woman stomped her high-heel clad foot, and Donna estimated her possible gossip was about twenty seconds from a full-blown snit. Since the platter ploy failed, another option had to be used. It was time to turn on the legendary southern charm that local residents were known for.

"Oh, you poor dear. That is *so* unfair. You come into the kitchen with me, and you can have your choice of desserts."

The woman nodded eagerly and followed Donna. When her two male companions tried to do likewise, Donna gave them the eye that had stopped doctors in their tracks. "You were not invited. The kitchen is a sacred sanctuary for women only."

If she had heard anyone else spout such drivel, she'd probably call the person a chauvinist. It did keep the men from following, though. Inside the sacred sanctuary sat another platter of goodies. This one had fruit skewers and chocolate-dipped strawberries. This was the *healthier* options tray.

Donna decided to make up another tray like the last because

what else would she be doing in the kitchen? "Take a look around and get what you want."

Following instructions, the tiny woman piled up quite a selection at one end of the island. When she tried to balance the haul to return to the dining room, Donna saw her informational opportunity leaving. Her favorite television private eye tried to stay as close to the truth as possible when soliciting information. It gave a nice feel of authenticity.

"Don't run off on me, honey. I don't get much girl talk. Pop a seat and tell me what's going on at the races. I was stuck here all day."

It was a last-ditch effort Donna didn't expect to work. To her surprise, the woman pulled out a stool and plopped down with a huge sigh and kicked off her shoes. "I needed a break anyway. I'm tired of being the rejected girlfriend of J.D. Sizemore."

Holy Toledo! Donna had hit the mother lode, but she needed to keep her talking. "Oh, sweetheart. I didn't catch your name."

"Tabitha, Tabitha Vorhees. I guess you haven't heard of me down here." She wrinkled her nose. "It may be a good thing."

Donna shrugged and gave her a sympathetic smile. "I'm not up with the young celebrity scene. So, why are you down here, again?"

"I keep asking myself that." Tabitha shrugged her shoulders as her gaze surveyed the kitchen. "Got any alcohol in here?"

Even though there was some cooking sherry and brandy for the flaming dishes in the cupboard, Donna said, "None here. Why don't you eat that chocolate-covered strawberry you have there? There might be a touch of alcohol in it." There wasn't.

"Okay." She popped the morsel into her mouth. "This *is* good." She reached for another one. "I could probably eat a dozen of these." She made a little sniff. "If I stuffed myself with another of these, I might forget my stupidity in agreeing to come down after J.D. gave me the heave-ho. Apparently, twenty-five is too old for J.D."

"How old is he?" Since Donna had heard the man was an important inventor of racing yachts, she assumed he was probably in his late forties, maybe fifties. He could be one of those guys who insisted on dating women young enough to be his granddaughter. She placed cheesecake wedges on small paper doilies while pretending not to have too much interest in the missing man's age.

"That's a hard one. He tried not to tell anyone. With the women, he wants them to think he was their age. With the older guys in the racing circuit, he wanted them to think he was younger than them so his success would really rub their noses in it."

She picked up a macaroon and gestured with it. "At the same time, he doesn't want to be considered *too* young. If he was just a kid, people would say he wouldn't last. He lies more about his age than any woman I know. One day, when we flew down to the islands, he took a business call and gave me his wallet and told me to rent a car."

The man was taking a chance handing off his wallet, especially if it was full of money. Still, Donna assumed J.D. must have trusted Tabitha not to grab the next flight and leave him. "What happened?"

"I rented a car, of course. Nothing special." She grimaced. "Car rental is limited in the islands. Mainly, all you get are aging sedans and often with a few scrapes on them."

Apparently, Tabitha lost track of where she was going with the conversation. "His age. Did you find out how old he was?" Donna asked to put her back on track.

"Thirty-five. That was almost a year ago. He should be thirty-six now."

Not as old as Donna expected. It made her wonder if that was

J.D.'s real driver's license. Fake ones were fairly easy to buy. Someone with the man's resources would have no trouble. The whole scenario of handing over his wallet smelled like a setup. Tabitha would look and share the information. Thirty-five would be a decent age for a yacht creator. It also wouldn't scare off the women too much. However, some might be open to a much older man, especially if they managed to weasel their way into the will.

"Hmm," Donna replied, deciding what question would serve her need to know who might want J.D. out of the picture. "Not too old. I'm surprised he thought you were too old. You're almost a decade younger."

"I know."

Tabitha played with a fruit skewer, pulling off the melon and pineapple and using the sharpened end to stab at a brownie. Donna could well imagine whom the brownie was a stand-in for.

"Remember, all the food you stab you have to eat."

Her guest complied, chomping down on the chocolatey goodness and rolling her eyes heavenward. "Yum!"

"Would you say J.D. got along well with people?" Donna considered this question better than her original one of who might want to kidnap or kill him. In the end, the guilty party wasn't always the most obvious one.

Tabitha continued to enjoy her bevy of sweet treats, making Donna think she hadn't heard her. Perhaps she needed something non-alcoholic to wash everything down with. A quick trip to the fridge netted her a bottle of organic milk, which she poured into a short glass. If her guest wasn't thirsty, she didn't want to waste it.

"Thanks." Tabitha took a long swig, leaving her with a milk mustache that made her look much younger than her quarter of a century years. She gave a long sigh before she started speaking. "J.D.

has charisma. He's exciting to be around. He was named one of the upcoming folks to watch in the yachting magazine. It's natural that people want to be near him. It's like he's that king that liked gold."

"Midas," Donna provided the name she felt Tabitha was searching for.

"Yeah, him, I think. Anyhow, everything he touches turns to gold. That's how J.D. seems. I kinda thought he was like that. Then I realized he manipulates people, events—just about everything to get his way. It doesn't matter who he steps on. If he's thrown you away, you're no longer valuable to him."

She pointed to herself with one manicured nail. "That's me. Not valuable."

"Oh, honey, that's not true." Donna was about to burst into an impassioned speech about women should not judge themselves by the value men place on them, but instead she said, "He's a jerk. You're better off without him."

"I know." There was a teary tone to her reply that had Donna moving around the island to put a comforting arm around Tabitha's shoulders. "Don't worry about him. A beautiful, talented woman like yourself can do anything she wants. Make him regret tossing you aside."

"You're right." Tabitha slid off the stool, bent down, levered on her heels, and wobbled a little as she stood. "That *is* the plan. In the end, I'm lucky to be rid of him. Too many other women are gunning for him. I don't want to get caught in the crosshairs."

Tabitha grabbed a few extra goodies, then swayed a little as she exited the kitchen. Donna stared at the closed door and mused on what was said. *Didn't want to get caught in the crosshairs.* It sounded like J.D. might not be too popular with everyone.

Chapter Twelve

THE SWISH OF the cat clock's tail accompanied Jasper's snores in the wee hours of the morning. Donna perched on a kitchen stool, nursing a cup of decaf and clicking through the various news reports of the missing tycoon, J.D. Sizemore. One account had him returning to the *mothership in the sky*. She could safely say that wasn't a valid lead. There were plenty of alleged friends who had both good and bad things to say about the man.

The women, a half-dozen artificially enhanced beauties, managed to mention their budding modeling or acting careers. One was clever enough to wear a T-shirt with her website emblazoned across her impressive chest. She got plenty of news coverage, but her attributes made the website difficult to read.

The women were cheerfully opportunistic, while the men tended to be a bit grimmer. A few went so far as to say J.D. got what he deserved. The big question was what had he got? No body, no declaration of drowning, foul play, or even kidnapping. It made her wonder if they knew something. Donna wrote down the names of the naysayers. With any luck, the men might be in the local area. She'd need to come up with a believable excuse to talk to them.

The clock clicked as the hour hand moved to one. Geez Louise, keeping her husband out all night would not accomplish what the twelve hours he'd already worked hadn't. Even the criminals must be in bed or at least most of them. As if on cue, the side door creaked open. Mark was home at last.

He plodded into the brightly lit kitchen and winced a little in the 100-watt intensity. The bulbs were special ordered to simulate sunlight. A cook needed to see what she was doing, and Donna would never admit she needed the extra illumination to read the tiny print on the ingredient packages. She slid off her stool to kiss him on the cheek. "Hi, honey. You hungry?"

He gave her a weary smile and cut his eyes to her coffee cup. "Decaf?"

"It is. There's some left for you. Want anything to go with that?" The doctor had put her husband on a limited coffee diet because the acid was eating away at his stomach. He had his one cup of caffeinated coffee before he left for work. Since Donna suspected he drank the sludge at the station that passed for coffee, she made sure his morning coffee was half decaf.

"I can eat. Any leftovers from the mixer?" He raised his bushy eyebrows as the smile lines in his face deepened.

"I wish. The regatta crowd is a hungry one. Cheap, too. At most of the mixers, we have guests who don't show. They instead decide to visit some of the local restaurants. A few bring back food, and then there are the ones who choose not to socialize. Every single guest showed, and you'd think they had been on a hunger strike before arriving. No worries. I did fix up some stroganoff. I had plenty of time to keep it warm while I was waiting for you."

"Donna, you know you don't have to wait up. You'll be getting up in a couple of hours to cook breakfast."

"I imagine you'll be up, too." She turned to retrieve the stroganoff that finally went into the fridge at midnight.

"Yes." He coughed, then cleared his throat. "I'm on duty as long as J.D. is missing. This is not the type of publicity Legacy needs:

Come to this coastal town and vanish forever." He held up his hands in a beseeching manner, then dropped them. Mark strolled to the counter, extracted a cup and poured himself some decaf before he took a seat.

The stroganoff was reheating in the microwave, which allowed ample time to query her husband about his day. "I thought you had a suspect, Jimmy Bobby."

"No." Mark grimaced. "Even though it seems almost impossible, the man knows less about the disappearance than I do. I was wondering if you'd call your mother and see what she knows about the family. Cecilia is a good source for local family information."

"Can do. Find out anything else?"

He gave his head a slow shake. "No one really liked J.D. They tried to hide it, not wanting to be a suspect, but it came out in so many ways. Sometimes, it was the way they said his name as if it were a foul taste they wanted to spit out. Other racers I spoke with practically twitched trying to suppress whatever unpleasant anecdote they might want to share. Their responses were short and useless. Things like, *I am familiar with the man, we didn't socialize,* and that's it. Nothing of use."

The microwave dinged. Donna retrieved the heated dinner and gathered silverware as she carried it to the island. "Here you go."

"Looks good and smells even better." Mark picked up a fork and dug in with gusto.

Donna mused aloud. It often helped her to find possible patterns. "Tabitha mentioned that J.D. Sizemore used people. Once he used them up, he threw them aside on his upward climb. Not too surprising that he doesn't have his own fan club."

"Who's Tabitha?" Mark asked with a loaded fork halfway to his mouth.

"J.D.'s old girlfriend."

Mouth full, Mark resorted to waggling his eyebrows. After a hard swallow, he remarked, "Leave it to you to sniff out a decent source while I'm out trying to chat up every closemouthed sailor in the county. How did you meet?"

Her husband's comment made her sit a little straighter. Praise from one of the best detectives in the county, and probably the state, was nothing to take lightly. While she enjoyed the impression that she was a full-out investigator, she knew better. Her ability to catch a bit of gossip or overheard conversation often made the difference between solving the case or not.

"She's a guest. A twig-like female that couldn't handle her wine. She dropped a wine glass."

"Oh." Mark winked. "Did you make her wash dishes to make up for it?"

Since Donna knew her husband was teasing, she stuck out her tongue at him. After he smirked, she decided to explain what really happened and her incredible machinations. "I was serving desserts from the platter à la waiter. I was hoping to hear some good gossip. All I got from Rosemarie was that Eugenia, the one who called the police on me for breaking into my own place, and her cohort, Cynthia, were really bold women who did what they wanted. I believe she admires them."

"Rosemarie?" Her husband queried.

Without her husband asking the question, she knew what he meant. Often, their minds were on the same mental tracks. "Oh, she moved into Tennyson's room. Real hard-luck story but she puts together a nice platter. An added plus is the guests like her. Anyhow, I was telling you about my devilishly clever plan to get Tabitha to gossip. Since she already had a bit to drink, I thought she'd be the best person."

Donna held out a flat hand as if carrying a platter. "I go out there with the sugar, and like a horde of locusts descending on me, they picked the dessert platter clean. Tabitha was so disappointed because she didn't get anything. Since she was the one, I wanted to talk to, I invited her into the kitchen for her pick of the sweets. For a tiny thing, she certainly stuffed herself. She was already feeling sorry for herself and let me know the type of person J.D. was. She implied he wasn't above doing the dirty deed to come out ahead. He probably *was* using a motor in a sail only race."

Mark put down his fork and whistled. "You amaze me. I'm glad you're on my side. Also, I'd like to talk to Miss Tabitha."

"I thought you would. She had more than her share of liquor. I suspect she has brought her own or was drinking before she got here."

"Probably the latter," Mark was quick to insert. "I guess I thought the regatta crowd would be the proper sort. Of course, there were lots of locals. Plenty of drinking going on, but no real fights, which is always a plus. The vendors with the beer wagons were the real winners today. However, it's late. Dinner was good, but we both need some shut-eye."

"Too true." Donna picked up the dirty dishes and placed them in the sink. "No reason for you to get up with the chickens. I guarantee Tabitha will be sleeping in."

"Ready?" Mark asked.

At Donna's nod, he turned off the kitchen lights, which caused a trio of night lights to pop on. On the other side of the kitchen door was a staff only sign, but a few guests still took midnight strolls. The nightlights helped them to discover, without knocking too much over, that the fridge was locked, as was the pantry.

★

A MOCKINGBIRD WELCOMED the dawn by going through its complete repertoire. Donna pulled a pillow over her head and groaned. Why couldn't birds get up later or at least be a bit quieter about it when they did? If the sun was up, she should be, too. Donna slid out of bed and turned off her alarm so as not to waken her sleeping husband. Apparently, he was able to sleep through nature's morning symphony.

After quietly dressing, she slipped out of the bedroom to start on breakfast. Donna pulled out the coffee and tea bar items to place in the dining room. There were always one or two early birds who were in search of their morning brew. She also had a plate of biscotti, along with a sign that noted breakfast would be served at nine. The sign was a result of a guest who complained all he got for breakfast was coffee and some dry toast sticks.

Coffee perking and a thermos of hot water by the tea service, Donna turned her attention to the kitchen. She turned on the oven to heat for her cheesy sausage and egg croissant casserole that she had put together previously and only had to bake. It took a solid hour to bake. Once she slid it into the oven, she poured herself a cup of coffee with plans to sit on the porch and enjoy a moment of peace before everyone woke up. This time of day the temperature was pleasant as opposed to sweltering.

Using her foot, she nudged her puggle, Jasper, awake. "Let's go."

Her dog opened one eye and gave her a look that expressed disbelief.

"I know good and well you've slept a solid ten hours."

The puggle gave an all-over stretch, then slowly stood, taking time to lift each leg as if checking their workability before stepping out of the bed. They made their slow way to the door. After one guest going crazy about a dog in the inn, Donna tried to keep Jasper's appearance very low-key. Most people never realized that the inn was Jasper's home.

At the front door, Donna struggled with the deadbolt as Jasper avidly sniffed the bottom of the door with his curly tail wagging wildly. Maybe her dog could smell a rabbit on the other side. With his partial beagle heritage, Jasper had an acute sense of smell.

Finally, she opened the door, only to have Jasper shoot through it. Since the wrought iron gate was closed, he pranced behind it, denied his prey. If there was a bunny out there somewhere, she doubted Jasper would actually hurt it. Donna placed her cup on the wicker table and turned to close the door. There was a white envelope taped to their door with cut-out letters that spelled out the word POLICE.

She knew well enough not to touch it. However, there was no reason not to inspect the envelope, which she felt sure was a kidnapping demand. The plain envelope was sold in bulk almost everywhere. With no writing on it anywhere, there wasn't much to distinguish it. Why would it be taped to the inn, unless someone knew a detective lived here? At least the message was getting out but not with the result she wanted. Her goal was for criminal types *not* to visit.

Something smelled like pomegranate and wax. She inhaled deeply, recognizing the candle scent. She had burned a couple at the Christmas Victorian tea. Why would a kidnapping demand smell like a holiday candle? As she pondered the possibility of a kidnapper with a preference for expensive, seasonal candles, Mark, still clad in his striped pajamas, pulled open the door, taking the envelope with it.

"What's Jasper barking at?"

Donna glanced over her shoulder to see her pup barking his head off. Funny, she hadn't noticed, so intent on the envelope. "I think he might be barking at the kidnappers or their messaging service."

Chapter Thirteen

THE MORNING SUNLIGHT struck the inn porch, spotlighting the two people on it. Mark sported classic bedhead with tufts of hair sticking up in disarray. Donna had already changed into her genial innkeeper look, complete with a ruffle gingham apron with appliquéd ducks and chicks on it. Jasper had given up following the unannounced visitors and trotted back to the porch.

"Strange." Mark stared at the envelope still attached to the door with the cut-out letters spelling police. "Who would know I lived here?"

Donna looked up from wrapping her apron around her right hand. "May I?" She brandished her apron wrapped hand.

"Go ahead," he gave a short nod.

After peeling the envelope off the door, Donna held it between two apron covered fingers. "I have latex gloves inside."

"Good." Mark held the door open for Donna and Jasper. The three of them trooped into the kitchen where Jasper pushed his food dish around, demanding breakfast.

"Geesh," Donna complained as she made her way to the cabinet to pull out a can of her fur baby's favorite grub. Her hubby immediately went to the cleaning closet and located latex gloves. He was going to open it without her.

"Wait!" she demanded. Jasper must have thought she was addressing him because his tail stopped wagging, and he sunk down into the saddest sit ever known to dogkind. "Not you."

She popped the can open and grabbed a fork to scrape the contents into the dish. Fortunately, her husband held the envelope in one gloved hand and a butter knife in the other. He was waiting for her. What a peach.

She straightened and strolled to the island to join her spouse. The smell of the cheesy breakfast casserole scented the air. Time was slipping by, and she had to get breakfast out. "Hurry! I have to start the bacon."

Mark raised his eyebrows, but thankfully did not comment. Instead, he inserted the butter knife and carefully sliced open the missive. He pulled out a piece of folded copy paper and opened it. Her hubby chose to read the large thirty sized font letters.

"We got the Sizemore guy. If you want him back, you need to pay us $100,000 in large bills. You have twenty-four hours. Leave money in blue trash can behind the baseball field at Legacy Junior High. Don't do anything stupid. The Kidnappers."

Weird. Donna shook her head. "They usually say, don't tell the police. They addressed the letter to the police as if they thought they might pay the ransom."

Mark made a non-committal reply as he picked up the letter to examine it more closely. Donna moved closer. A colored smear soiled part of the letter. "Look."

"I see it."

Donna leaned forward and sniffed, earning a curious glance from her husband.

"What are you doing?"

"Checking out the smear. I'm pretty sure it's from one of those expensive candles they sell at the designer mall. I noticed the smell outside. It's a winter scent, which is out of place now."

"Interesting." Mark carefully folded the note and placed it back into the envelope. "I'll need a plastic bag. Looks like I'll be heading in to work early."

A throat clearing caused the two of them to look up toward the back hallway where Rosemarie stood. She smiled and waved by wiggling the fingers on her upraised hand. "Morning, everyone. I figured there were things you might want me to do."

"You're so right. Please start in the dining room. Make sure it's clean after last night and put the white tablecloths on the tables. You'll find them in the buffet cabinet. Then put the napkin wrapped silverware at each setting."

"Okay," she cheerfully agreed and headed in to the dining room.

Donna stared at the closed interior door with pursed lips before asking, "Do you think she heard?"

"Hard to say." Mark shrugged. "I'm more upset at being caught in my pajamas." He took the offered plastic bag, slipped the envelope into it, and took it with him as he left to dress.

No time to speculate, Donna hauled out the cast iron skillet to fry up some thick-cut bacon. The problem with the breakfast menus was deciding if the guests expected a big Southern breakfast or something a little more gourmet. Bacon was usually a prerequisite except when there were vegans in the house. Good thing Maria had included on the application that special diets would require notification beforehand.

Her mind continued to ponder the envelope as she put together a tray of juices, ice water, and milk for Rosemarie to carry out. Usually, it was help yourself when it came to drinks. The breads were placed in a basket on the table while Donna delivered the hot entrées.

If a person went to the trouble to deliver a ransom demand to the inn, it meant they knew a police officer lived there. Could be they might even know his name but didn't have enough letters to spell it out. They also might not want to take a chance of dropping off a letter at the police station.

Donna placed the breakfast rolls, croissants, and pastries on a large cookie sheet. The heating stones she placed in the baskets to keep the bread warm she put directly on the rack. Rosemarie popped back into the kitchen.

Donna pointed to the tray. "Put out the juice glasses. They're in the tall cabinet in the dining room. If they want more, they can get it. If you put out water glasses, fill them. That will keep folks from using them to guzzle a carton of OJ."

A giggle greeted the instructions. Her absurdly happy helper said, "Got it." She picked up the tray and turned to leave, but added, "I'm surprised the kidnappers asked for so little. Maybe Sizemore has money problems."

Well, well, it seemed like Rosemarie showed up just in time to eavesdrop. Mark wouldn't be very pleased. "Ah, let's keep this between us."

It was hard for Donna to know if she should even mention it to her husband before he left. It wasn't like it would change anything. Besides, he was already running on nerves with all the news organizations putting their focus on Legacy and not in a good way. Maybe she'd mention it after they rescued Sizemore. Come to think of it, the letter didn't mention anything about returning the tycoon. She'd need to point that out to her husband. It may be a vital clue.

The oven buzzer sounded. Donna switched out the casserole, which she covered and left on top of the stove to insert the bread and heating stones. Another stove, or at least an oven, would be helpful. Even though the kitchen was sizable, after replacing the fridge with a professional one and a restaurant dishwasher, there wasn't much room left. What she needed was one of those stoves that had an extra oven, like her mother had back in the day.

Her eyebrows shot up with the mental mention of her mother. The stove was definitely history, but maybe her mother could come babysit the inn for the afternoon, which would allow Donna to do a little nosing around. Why should Mark have all the fun?

Her husband entered the room clutching a mug of coffee he must have obtained from the coffee bar in the dining room. "Anything ready?"

"Breakfast casserole, some bacon."

"Sounds good. Could you put it between two pieces of toast for a meal on the go?" He shot her such an engaging smile that Donna decided not to point out why it wouldn't be practical. She even did him the courtesy of not pointing out his cardiologist was not a fan of eating on the run. For that matter, the doctor would not be a fan of bacon, either.

After putting two thick slices of multi-grain bread in the toaster, Donna cut a wedge of casserole and carefully sliced it, making it do-able for sandwich filler. She topped it with bacon but went to the fridge for a spread to hold it together. "Mustard?"

"Sounds good."

He sipped his coffee as Donna created a monster sandwich which might be the only decent meal her sweetheart would have all day. "Did you notice there was no mention of returning Sizemore?"

"I did. Was wondering when you would notice. I'm going to have the lab examine it. There are so many possibilities, such as Sizemore being already dead. It could be a bogus letter from someone playing a prank. It also may be used to throw us off. There was one dude who even faked his death. I'm leaning toward that one. What would his motivation be?"

Donna reached for a napkin to wrap around the sandwich. "Could be money. Maybe he isn't as rich as everyone thinks he is. He could have a major life insurance policy, but who benefits and how would he get his hands on the money?"

"Yeah," Mark exhaled through pursed lips. "The case gets harder instead of easier. Where are my informants who want to tell all?"

She held up one finger, knowing she could definitely help with that.

"No," Mark said emphatically. He gave her a peck on the cheek. "You know the protocol. I can't ask a citizen for help."

She knew, but it wasn't going to stop her. He knew that, too.

Chapter Fourteen

CAR DOORS SLAMMING, loud conversation, and laughter drew Donna to her bedroom window. She'd retreated to her room to call her mother. No reason to test Rosemarie's eavesdropping skills. As far as Donna could tell, they were in fine shape. Aware the rooms weren't soundproof, she decided to turn on the television—except there was no remote. She'd forgotten that she'd played musical remotes, and she still had the gum encrusted one stuck in the back pocket of her dirty jeans. TVs do have manual controls on the side or front.

Another thing she needed to get done today. It wasn't like she had any top-secret info to relay to her mother. Besides, she'd sent Rosemarie upstairs to fill the pantry. The woman probably struck up a conversation with a guest. Donna punched in her mother's number. By the third ring, she was considering hanging up when a breathless Cecilia picked it up.

"What do you need?"

"That's not a very loving way to talk to your only daughter."

When Donna opened the inn, she had been rather close-mouthed with her mother, knowing her parent would offer advice where none was wanted. Running a bed and breakfast turned out to be more work than she expected, which meant she occasionally had to ask for help from her opinionated parent.

Cecilia sighed. "You're right. I'm having some issues cornering

Loralee. She has a grooming appointment today."

"I understand," Donna said as she mentally reviewed what else her mother might be doing. "Are you using Bill's Pet Wash and Grooming?"

"I have to. Bill's is the only place willing to take a basset hound. The other salons groom small dogs. Most of my purses are bigger than they are.

"Great." Bill's was only a half-mile from the inn. "I'm sure you don't want to wait around for her, either."

"There's no matter of wanting. I can't just leave her there all day. I need to be in the vicinity when Bill calls."

"Why not come over here? Mark had some matters he wanted me to ask you about, anyhow. I could make you a cup of cappuccino."

"You don't have to bribe me to visit my only daughter. I'll be there in three shakes of a lamb's tail. I still want the cappuccino and shortbread to go with it. Bye."

"Bye," Donna echoed her mother's word then stared at the phone. Geesh, did she only call her mother when she needed something? Better send her flowers to make up for all the inn-related favors.

Since she couldn't dart out of the door when her mother showed up, Donna decided to head in to the kitchen to whip up shortbread. It would be hard for her mother to turn her down after she made her cookies. The extras could go into the pantry baskets for the guests.

While the oven had reached the desired temperature, Donna creamed the butter and sugar together as she considered the ransom note. It was peculiar. Basically, it was a demand for money with no mention of releasing the racing yacht tycoon. Thinking of the note reminded her she'd left her cup outside on the porch which was not a good look for the inn.

Donna put the spoon down and hurried to get her forgotten coffee cup. No wonder she had been a bit crabby—she hadn't even had time for her first cup of java. On the wicker side table sat her coffee with an oily sheen on top.

If she was going to tidy up the porch, she should make sure to get everything. She strolled down the length of the porch, making a note to water the ferns. Nothing to be picked up so far but as she drew closer to the front door, a tiny speck of color caught her eye.

"Aha!" Donna scooped it up. No random trash, no matter how small, was going to litter her porch. She held up the colorful wrapper scrap from a popular children's candy. She pocketed the offending piece and made sure to grab her cup.

Back in the kitchen, she washed her hands and went back to making cookies. Just as she slid the first pan into the oven, a long baying howl came from outside, causing Jasper to lift his ears. It was almost as if he said *is that who I think it is?* A second bay confirmed it. Jasper jumped to his feet and barked back. The side door opened. A scratching of dog nails on linoleum was accompanied by her mother's sensible heels footsteps. In Donna's opinion, no heels were sensible, but her mother was a product of her generation and never left the house without putting on her face and her heels.

"Yoo-hoo, sweetie!" her mother called. As she entered the kitchen, a large black and white basset hound swirled about her feet, delighting Jasper, who greeted the canine with even more barking and vigorous tail wagging.

Donna eyed the hound that was about as graceful as an elephant doing ballet. Some of her guests were not animal fans and had some issues with the more discreet Jasper. Thank goodness most of them had left to secure good seats for the regatta.

"Hi, Mom. I thought Loralee had a grooming appointment." Donna flicked on the cappuccino machine and removed a white cup from the cabinet. She added the instant coffee granules, a hot chocolate package, and a tablespoon of the coffee creamer sugar mixture she used for the machine. The cinnamon and nutmeg canisters Donna put on the island since her mother preferred to handle that step herself.

"Yeah. That's what I thought, too. When I arrived at Bill's there was a note on the door that read *Family Emergency, Please Reschedule.*"

"You'd think he could have called." Donna started the machine, drowning out her mother's reply. "What did you say?"

Cecilia arched her eyebrows and slowly enunciated each word. "He isn't good with technology. That's why he works with animals."

"It's a phone for Pete's sake. They've been around for a century or more."

Cecilia shrugged her shoulders. "Bill is good with Loralee. I can overlook a few quirks. What matter does Mark want me to look into?" She rubbed her hands together in anticipation. "Just think, I'm already working for Legacy's finest, and it took you how long to be considered a consultant?"

Donna placed the brimming cup in front of her mother and ignored the dig. Her mother knew she wasn't a consultant. "This is unofficial, of course. Think of yourself as an informant."

"Hmm, informant." Cecilia twisted off the lids of the spice containers and liberally dosed the beverage. "Not sure if I like the sound of that. It sounds seedy."

"It isn't. Mark's not asking you to rat on the mob. He just wants to know what you know about the Burdan family, especially Thelma and Jimmy Bobby."

"Woo-wee! That family is Legacy's own little Peyton Place." She took a sip of her beverage and mulled the matter over. "I'm sure I need a cookie as payment."

Donna placed one hand on her hip. "You're worse than a kid. They're in the oven. I made them special just for you."

"That's why I mentioned it."

"I imagine you could tell me a little without a cookie."

"I could." Cecilia's lips tipped up into a sly smile. "However, if I did, it would set a precedent. You'd be expecting information without payment. I already missed out on the fifty dollars the tip line promises for information leading to a conviction."

The oven buzzer sounded, preventing Donna from getting into a prolonged discussion about the fact that having colorful parents doesn't necessarily turn you into a criminal. "There they are. Your payment is coming."

"You make the best shortbread cookies."

Donna used her spatula to move the cookies from the pan to the cooling rack. She placed two on a saucer and carried it to her mother. She felt the need to respond to the cookie comment. "It's all the love I put into them."

Jasper rubbed against one leg, hoping for a handout while Loralee used her imploring eyes to beg.

Cecilia snatched up the still-warm cookie and bit into it. "It's the butter that makes it so good. You don't skimp on the butter. You use the Irish kind, right?"

"You know the rules. You can eat all you want, but you aren't getting your hands on my recipes."

"I'm blood."

"That you are. I also know you have no intention of cooking. You'd just hand it over to one of your friends. Before I know it, my special shortbread recipe would be in the hands of a competitor." To demonstrate she wasn't playing, Donna folded her arms.

"You can be just like your father sometimes."

If that was supposed to be an insult, Donna didn't feel it. Her father often gave in to his wife, but there were times when he refused to be moved. It sounded more and more like a compliment. "Peyton Place," she prompted.

Cecilia reached for another cookie and nibbled the edge of it as if trying to make it last. Finally, she waved her cookie as she spoke. "Irma and Joe Bob weren't bad people on their own."

"I assume they're the parents."

"They are. Normally when folks marry, they pick someone who brings out the best in them. Surely Irma must have misunderstood and thought she was supposed to marry someone who brought out the worst. Most folks felt sorry for the children because they assumed the parents were always on the edge of divorce, but it never happened until Irma won the lottery. It was only around ten thousand, but she refused to share with Joe Bob. If anyone thought things were ugly before, they had no clue how much uglier they'd get. The kids were grown and had moved out. Joe Bob took up with a drifter to prove to Irma he didn't need her or her lottery winnings. Irma headed to Mexico where her money would last longer. The town is quieter with both of them gone."

The story fit with the one Thelma told Donna. "What about the kids? How did they turn out?"

Her mother's eyes rolled up as if she was mentally opening and closing drawers in a file cabinet marked Legacy's inhabitants. "Okay. Better than you'd expect with the family life they had. The brother and sister are pretty tight."

"Would you call them honest?"

"I would. Jimmy Bobby has been through a number of jobs but hasn't found his niche yet. None of his bosses badmouthed him, so that makes him the decent sort."

Pretty much the same as Mark said. "Your son-in-law will be glad to hear that. He likes any information that lines up with his opinion."

"I can understand that." Cecilia pushed the now empty plate toward Donna in a very unsubtle clue. "Did you watch the movie about those kid detectives?"

Donna paused for a moment, then exclaimed, "Wait, that's it!" The information had been there all along, just out of reach. "I bet the kidnappers watched that movie, too."

Chapter Fifteen

THE OVEN HEATED up the kitchen while the aroma of baking butter, sugar, and flour scented the air. There was the underlying smell of cappuccino, but in a scent war, shortbread won hands down. Donna maneuvered one pan of delicately toasted cookies out of the oven, onto the counter, and inserted another pan of cookies to bake.

She cut her eyes to her mother, who was sipping her beverage but with a gleam in her eye. Geesh, leave it to her parent to hear everything. Weren't the elderly supposed to have bad hearing? Not her mother—the woman could probably hear a pin drop during a gale. Donna couldn't believe she'd said *kidnappers* in front of her. Cecilia wasn't a gossip, but she could be nosy and possibly imagined herself as an amateur sleuth. It wasn't hard to see that the apple did not fall far from the tree when it came to Donna's deductive skills. Right now, she needed to distract her mother from the subject at hand.

High heeled footsteps clattered on the inn's hardwood staircase. It had to be Tabitha since almost everyone else had already left. Besides, she doubted any of the remaining guests would be wearing high heels for a day at the beach. Only a woman who wanted to prove she was not devastated over being tossed aside would go to the trouble to gussy up on the slightest chance of being seen. Donna needed to talk to her since Mark hadn't had the chance.

Outside, there was the sound of a vehicle with a wonky transmission that had Donna stripping off her hot pad mittens and peering out the kitchen window. "It's Thelma. She's probably here with another prediction."

"Sounds interesting," Cecilia cooed. "Does she use Tarot cards?"

A steady *tap-tap* of footsteps headed to the front door. "I'm going to let you handle Thelma. I need to talk to Tabitha before she leaves."

Donna darted out the kitchen door before her quarry escaped. Just as she thought, the woman was done up to the nines with her hair artfully tousled that Donna knew probably took a hairdryer, flat iron, curling iron, and multiple styling products to achieve. Complicated hair rituals were for the young or people who had much more time than Donna did.

"Tabitha! Wait."

The willowy woman turned, revealing an artfully painted lower half of her face and sunglasses. "Yes? Can I help you?"

Tabitha exuded the frosty civility of a celebrity recognized in public. She acted like she didn't even recognize Donna.

"It's me. The person who escorted you into my kitchen sanctuary and plied you with an assortment of desserts."

Instead of replying, Tabitha pulled down her glasses with her index finger until they were perched on the end of her nose. "Oh, it *is* you."

As a detective, Mark had a reason to question the woman. For Donna, it was hard to know how to proceed. Before she could say anything, a firm knock on the front door resonated. The beveled side panel windows revealed Thelma and an unknown child that made Donna cringe just thinking what damage the little darling could do.

Cecilia popped out of the kitchen as if a wind-up doll to answer the door. In an inspired move, Donna gently herded Tabitha into the kitchen. "I just made some shortbread cookies and want you to try one. I value your opinion."

"All right," Tabitha agreed. "Just one. I ate too much last night."

"How about a cappuccino to go with it?" Donna suggested, well aware it would take time to make the beverage and a little more to consume it. Tabitha sucked her lips in as if to stop herself from agreeing to the calorie-rich drink.

Observing her indecision, Donna said, "I'll go ahead and make two. I just hate to drink alone."

"But the…"

Knowing her reservations about the calories and her desire to keep her waif-like figure, it was time to improvise or as it was better known, *making harmless stuff up.* "If you stand while eating or drinking something, it goes straight through your digestive tract without you gaining an ounce. That's why it's so bad to eat while watching television since people are always sitting and the weight gets stuck right in the middle."

The sheer idiocy of her statement made Donna wince, especially when she heard the high-pitched squeal in the foyer. She held onto a cabinet handle to prevent herself from darting out the door to see what was happening. If her mother managed to raise both her and her brother, she should be able to handle one child.

"I never knew that!" Tabitha said with obvious glee and removed her sunglasses. I'll need to be standing all the time."

Guilt perched on Donna's shoulders like an oversized albatross. It was the nonsense women said to each other to give them permission to enjoy a treat now and then. It was up there with any food consumed after midnight over a kitchen sink didn't count. Even if the woman did put on a few ounces, she'd probably only go up to size zero. According to current social media, curvy was in, which meant she would be doing the woman a favor.

Donna pointed to her own waistline. "See? Lots of sitting on the couch and watching television and snacking."

"Obviously…" Tabitha agreed without any argument, which irritated Donna. Sure, she had been slimmer in the past, but she wasn't *that* big. Still, pride had to be shelved for the sake of information.

"So, where were you off to before I interrupted?" Donna inquired as she poured the ingredients into the cappuccino machine.

"Nowhere special. I'll tell you where I wasn't going. The races. I'm tired of everyone giving me funny looks."

"Why would they do that?" Her finger hovered above the start button, waiting for an answer before she started the noisy device.

Tabitha sighed. "You know. They think I had something to do with the boat crashing and J.D.'s disappearance."

The whine of the machine cut off conversation. If Donna announced she was going to make cappuccinos, she needed to do so. Once the frothy coffee concoction finished, she poured it into a stoneware mug and handed it to Tabitha.

Even though Mark wasn't a fan of ambush-style questioning, Donna had gotten results in the past. She waited until her guest sipped the beverage and made an appreciative sound.

"Everyone thinks *you* did it? Why would they think that?" Donna didn't expect much besides protestations that she didn't do it which would lead to an invitation to help find who did.

Tabitha took another sip and sat down on a stool, indicating the seriousness of what she had to say. There was a plate of shortbread cookies on the island. She reached for one and bit into it. "I had no reason to want to hurt J.D. My brothers think they convinced me to come to the regatta to show everyone I wasn't broken up over being dumped. My go-to attitude was supposed to act like I didn't care. My real goal was to get back with J.D. I'm not even sure why he broke up with me."

She shrugged her shoulders. "I wasn't demanding. Not like some of his previous women were. Always wanting the expensive stuff, extravagant vacations and all. No, I wasn't like that. On our last trip to the islands, we flew comfort class."

Since Donna had never made her way *out* of coach, comfort class sounded pretty nice to her.

Tabitha's face puckered up as if she might cry, but she continued talking. "J.D. is a proud man. He put everything into the *Foam Empress*, and he had to win. If he did, it would be the boost his business needed. Once he got back into the money and the winner's circle, he would stare out into the stands and see me: the woman who always supported him."

Wait a minute. Last night, she'd basically told Donna what a cheating, conniving rat J.D. was. Suddenly, he was the underdog, and Tabitha was his cheerleader. Was this the story she came up with to deflect guilt from herself? "Basically, you're saying you would never hurt him?"

"No." She picked up her cup and took another sip. "I know nothing about sailing. If I ever had to hurt him, I had another plan."

"Which is?" Donna asked as she took the stool across from the jilted girlfriend.

"Oh no." She shook one coral tipped finger. "You have to get your *own* plan."

"Fair enough," Donna agreed nonchalantly and reached for a shortbread cookie. Had the woman confessed to having a plan to embarrass the man, such as posting unflattering photos online, or did she have something more devious in mind? The sound of retreating footsteps and her mother bidding Thelma goodbye meant she only had a little time left before Cecilia invited herself into the conversation. "Wouldn't you like people to think you're not guilty?"

"Yes." Tabitha gave a little sniff and rolled her eyes. "You know how people are. They enjoy seeing people suffer. There's a German word that describes it. Scatty Frog, I think."

When words failed her, Donna had to put her hand over her face. Tabitha must mean *schadenfreude*, which referred to taking enjoyment from other people's misery. Personally, she would have called them *petty*. Once she had her expression under control, she dropped her hand.

"What you need to do is help find J.D. to prove you had nothing to do with the accident. Think about how grateful J.D. would be, too. He'd want to do something extra special for you since you were the only woman who tried to find him"

"Oh?" Tabitha responded, her eyebrows arching once she caught Donna's meaning. "What can I do? I don't even know where he is."

"Neither does anyone else." Donna waited a few beats, using Mark's technique of not talking to introduce expectancy and tension. Mentally, she counted up to five Mississippis before continuing. "We could track him with a dog, but we would need a personal item from J.D. that had his scent on it. Would you have anything like that?"

Tabitha put a finger up to her lips as she considered the question. "I think I might."

Chapter Sixteen

DONNA FOLLOWED TABITHA upstairs to retrieve whatever the item was that carried J.D.'s scent. From her position on the second-floor landing, she spotted sunshine and blue skies outside. The innkeeper-turned-sleuth took a moment to appreciate the boon the weather was to the race. Good weather, more watchers, and possibly more money in local pockets. With any luck, whatever souvenir Tabitha packed could possibly help locate the missing millionaire.

Her guest unlocked the room door and pushed it wide. "Come on in. I'll get the tie."

Odd. Donna wouldn't have suspected a tie as a sentimental item. Maybe the woman really did care about J.D. as opposed to it being a story to deflect guilt. She stepped only a foot into the room, though not out of courtesy. Every inch of the floor was covered with discarded clothing, cosmetics, and shoes. Donna didn't remember her bringing that many suitcases, either. "I'll stay right here."

"Oh, yeah." Tabitha giggled. "I tend to nest." She carefully picked her way through the mess, talking as she did so. "I bought J.D. an Armani tie for his birthday. Spent a couple of hundred bucks on it. You might think to look at me that I come from money. I don't. I work in a boutique and met J.D. when he came in to buy a gift for his then current girlfriend."

The more Donna heard about J.D., the less she liked him. Tabitha rambled on about her romance with J.D., listing all the great gestures, including helicopter trips and limo rides. It was starting to grate. Somehow Donna felt sympathy for the previous girlfriend who was put aside by a random stranger. It was probably inevitable. Still, she felt for the unknown woman.

Clothing flew through the air as Tabitha muttered to herself. "I know it's here. I thought I could take it back to my shop and resell it, if nothing else."

There went the thought that Tabitha held onto the tie for sentimental purposes.

Meanwhile, who knew what Thelma told her mother? If it was useful information, her mother might already be in her car, trying to track down the kidnappers or on the phone, calling in favors. Donna shifted her weight from foot to foot which was the best she could do in the tiny area of cleared space. "Are you sure the tie was even used? It needs to have J.D.'s smell on it."

"No worries." Tabitha giggled again. "It has J.D. all over it. I planned to wash it if I put it back in the store."

Donna held up her hand. "No details needed."

"Aha! I found it." Tabitha brandished a sandwich baggie with a rolled-up swath of burgundy and gold.

"I'll take it." Donna held out her hand to accept the bag and pocketed it. Not wanting to grab useful deductive tools and dash, she added, "I hope you have a lovely day today. I have some gift cards downstairs that might be useful. Good for a few restaurants and coffee shops. I even have free admission to the Columbus Days Museum."

"Columbus Days?" Tabitha's eyebrows shot up.

"It's a thing around here," Donna said, uncertain she wanted to explain their local festival that celebrated Christopher Columbus crashing one of his ships off their coast. The historical figure spent just enough time ashore to board another one of his ships and sail home. No one could even verify it even happened, but it was enough reason for a tall ships parade and folks dressing up as pirates. Never mind that Columbus wasn't a pirate. "On second thought, you might want to skip the museum."

Tabitha shrugged her shoulders. "No problem. I'm not much of a museum girl." She wrinkled her nose and tapped a finger against her cheek. "However, I might consider it if I thought no one else was going to be there. I'm tired of people gawking at me and whispering. Some don't bother to even whisper."

"The ticket will be downstairs. I'll put it and the gift cards on the entrance table. Gotta go."

She had a hard time reading the woman. At one point she thought she was just another trust-fund baby who filled her life with parties, vacations, and events. When she discovered Tabitha was a shop-girl with dreams of grandeur, it made Donna feel a little sympathy for her. Some might call her a gold digger, but she could be just a woman dazzled by a chance to experience how the rich lived. To such a woman, an Armani tie meant a lot.

Donna patted her pocket. "I'll bring it back when I'm done."

"Thank you." Tabitha's attitude of being a self-assured beauty slipped a little as her hand slipped from her face to her side. When she turned to face Donna, there was a glassy sheen to her eyes. "You've been really nice to me. Nicer than anyone has been in a long time."

Many labels had been attached to Donna, including hardworking, practical, stubborn, and even nosy. It was not very often people called her nice or kind. Warmth enveloped her, causing her to spontaneously step forward and hug Tabitha. "Don't you worry.

Everything will work out."

"I know," Tabitha swallowed.

Donna dropped her arms and took a step backward, embarrassed at her impulsiveness. "I'll put the gift cards on the table."

Before she could do something else awkward, Donna turned and hustled downstairs. So much to do. By the time she hit the landing, she paused for just a moment. Had she just been conned? The glassy eyes did her in, but all good con artists could cry on cue. Maybe the shop girl's story was a lie. It wasn't like she could ask her mother to investigate Tabitha's background. With that thought, she went in search of her mother after putting the gift cards and museum tickets on the foyer table.

The kitchen was her first stop where she found her mother enjoying another cappuccino. "There you are. What did Thelma want?" Remembering the child, she added, "You had the kid in sight at all times?"

Her mother rolled her eyes. "You'd think I had never been around children before. I had two, remember?"

"I know." While her mother never seemed to dislike her maternal duties, she loved to reflect on her and her brother's childhood. In her tales, they were mischievous imps."

A streamer of smoke crept out from the oven along with an acrid odor, spurring Donna into action. She ran to the stove, pulling the oven door open and allowing even more smoke to barrel out which set off the fire alarm. "Doggone it!"

She pulled out the cookie sheets that featured the darkened remnants of what was left of the shortbread with bare hands. "Ouch!"

She put the oven mitts on as an afterthought. The alarm continued to shriek, and Jasper decided to join in by baying and was aided by Loralee. Instead of helping by settling her own dog, her mother placed her hands over her ears.

"Donna, do something!"

That's the problem with being responsible. Everyone expected you to solve the issues. Donna scraped the burnt cookies into the trash and carried the cookie sheet in one hot pad mittened hand into the foyer where the smoke alarm was located. She waved it vigorously under the alarm until it stopped. Jasper was still baying, though.

"Stop it!"

Donna walked back into the kitchen and glared at Jasper, who immediately stopped baying. Her mother dropped her hands from her ears. "It's about time."

Nothing seemed to be working out this morning. She gestured to the oven. "Why couldn't you take out the cookies from the oven? I made them for you."

"I enjoyed my two." She patted her stomach. "I couldn't eat another. Have to watch my weight. Simon and I are planning a vacation."

Her mother's new husband was big on planning exotic getaways. "You're not planning on wearing one of those tiny bikinis, are you?"

"Shut your mouth." Her mother's face puckered up as she tried not to laugh. "Besides, I did what you told me to do. Checked out Thelma and Jimmy Bobby's family. As pathetic and colorful as expected. The kids seemed to be the most normal of the bunch and that isn't saying much. Still, they're decent enough. In fact, Thelma came by to warn you not to do anything. She had asked for your help earlier, but now she told me there was a black cloud hanging over you and you're in danger."

Donna snorted. Sometimes, she did feel as if there was a black cloud hovering close by. "Was that all she had to say?"

"Pretty much." Cecilia nodded her head. "She kept emphasizing it as if I needed help understanding that my only daughter could be in danger."

"I think I'm fine. Don't worry too much. The day J.D. vanished, she showed up and told me murder was in the air or something like that. At this point, no bodies have been found. It looks more like kidnapping or an attempt to fake his death."

"Hmm," Cecilia murmured. "Faking death is always a possibility, especially if the man had money issues."

"I thought of that," Donna remarked as she plopped down on an island stool, already weary before lunchtime. The kid detective movie featured children solving the case of a missing dog that had been kidnapped by the bad guys. Inept baddies melted wax on their fingers to obscure their fingerprints on their ransom note, which resulted in smears, and the kids solved the case by tracing the type of wax. "Do you think any adults watched that movie?"

"We did."

"True enough. I better call Mark." It may or may not help. It could be that her note writers made a mistake somewhere and left a print. Then again, maybe Jasper held a clue.

Chapter Seventeen

A FAT, RED squirrel ran across the inn's front porch and had the nerve to stop in full view of the kitchen window and chatter. Most people might consider the behavior peculiar. Donna didn't. It had happened way too much lately with the same results. The squirrel, which Mark had named Mr. McNutty, was Jasper's personal nemesis. The aging and slightly overweight puggle had no chance of catching the swift creature. It didn't stop him from trying, though. Mostly, it resulted in a barking frenzy.

Donna held her cell up to her ear, listening to it ring and hoping her dog didn't notice the bushy-tailed rodent taunting him. She really needed to get ahold of Mark. The wax smears might not mean anything. It did seem curious that the scented wax ransom note arrived after a movie showed that featured using wax to disguise fingerprints. Personally, she felt almost any run-of-the-mill kidnapper would use latex gloves, which was both neater and simpler.

The phone rang again, which wasn't good. If it went into voice mail, the chances of Mark calling her back in a timely fashion weren't fantastic. No response or a late reply meant things were crazy at work.

"Hello?" Mark gasped the word.

Jasper moved his head the tiniest bit and noticed his furry antagonist and charged the window, barking as he did so.

Great. Here, Donna thought the extra tall windows were an asset. She covered her free ear with one hand, hoping to tone down the barking as she walked away from Jasper and into the foyer. It would be no use telling him to calm down as long as Mr. McNutty was outside.

"Mark. I'm so glad I reached you." There was the sound of yelling in the background and what sounded like car doors. "I needed to talk to you about the ransom note and the movie it's from."

Someone at the other end of the phone yelled Mark's name. "I don't have time for a movie review. What about the note?"

The front door opened and the two male guests who had called the inn *quaint* earlier, entered. Donna paused, not willing to discuss the case in front of them. They paid little attention to her as they walked past her, deep into their own conversation.

"I can't believe you forgot the sunscreen," the taller one said.

"It's not my job to protect your lily-white skin. You should have thought of it yourself. You're a walking poster child for sunburn prevention."

Donna moved back into the kitchen where Jasper was now growling at McNutty. He could erupt into full barks at any moment, which forced her to slide into the basement and close the door behind her. No reason to turn on the light because she didn't expect to be there long. "There was a movie about kid detectives."

"The note, please. We're setting up for the drop right now."

"You don't even know if it *is* a bonafide note." Her husband had noticed the same discrepancies she had. She added, "They didn't even mention a getaway vehicle, such as a helicopter."

"It's not like they're holed up somewhere and are trying to shoot their way out. What about the note? Running low on time. We're going to make the drop and watch who comes to get it, nabbing the lawbreaker who would try and ruin Legacy's first regatta." There was more yelling in the background. "Be there in a minute!"

Donna knew he wasn't addressing her, but it did let her know how close the conversation was to ending. "In the movie, the bad guys put wax on their fingers to hide their fingerprints. It ended up making smears on the paper, just like the ransom note taped to the door. The movie was shown last week."

Mark remarked, "Stupid thing to do."

"I thought so, too. Did the lab find any fingerprints?"

"No. That's why we resorted to paying the ransom."

Legacy was a defunct textile mill town that had turned to tourism to boost its bottom line. The various antique shops, unique restaurants, and inns such as her own brought in some folks. Not nearly enough, though, which is why the town grabbed on hard to every opportunity that presented itself from Gen Con to a televised baking show. While the various opportunities had helped, there wasn't an excess of cash floating around.

"Where's the ransom money coming from?"

"Fake. We cut paper that is similar in weight to the real thing. We have some actual money on top that we borrowed from the evidence locker. We don't intend to let whoever picks it up to even have a chance to open the case. We're moving out. Bye."

The phone disconnected before Donna could say bye. She stared at the phone, wondering how much danger Mark would be in. It wasn't like he'd be alone. The majority of Legacy's force were probably in on this one operation with a skeleton crew watching the regatta crowd. After all, the bad thing had already happened with the favored-to-win boat wiping out and its owner vanishing.

As much as she hated to admit it, maybe her mother was right about J.D. staging his own death. It had happened before and not too far from Legacy, either. Some financier who took a bunch of trusting souls' money parachuted out of his own plane and allowed it to ditch in the ocean. The swindler was later spotted at an RV park, proving that campers still watched the news.

While her husband hoped to spring a trap on the kidnappers, the very least she could do was check out J.D.'s boat for clues. Sure, the police had been over it at least once, possibly more than once. The difference was she had a plan. The plan was quite clever if she said so herself. Not only would Mark be proud of her, but the commissioner would also have to admit that certain civilians could be a major help to crime investigations.

All Donna had to do was explain to her mother what she needed to do. Nothing big, just answer any questions a guest might have. Cecilia would have to check the rooms Rosemarie cleaned and possibly assist. When all the rooms were booked, it could be a big job. It made her wonder how the maids in the chain hotels did so many rooms.

Mind on her plan, Donna went in search of her mother, who had gone upstairs to fill the snack pantries. She also had mentioned to look in on Rosemarie. Yesterday, the woman was a bundle of energy. Still, that could have been just to impress her. Some people became better workers as time went on. Life experience taught her otherwise. Most people discovered what was the littlest they could get by with and did that instead.

She could hear voices as she ascended the stairs, and it wasn't her sunscreen couple.

"What were you doing in her room?" Cecilia's familiar voice inquired.

If Donna had ears more like Jasper's, they would have perked up. Even though Cecilia's tone sounded pleasant and non-committal, Donna heard the underlying disbelief in it. She had been on the losing side of such inquiries as a kid and knew how they went. Her mother usually asked questions about things even though she already knew the answer.

"I was cleaning," Rosemarie insisted, although she did sound a tad defensive.

"There was a Do Not Disturb sign on the door."

"Hoo, boy!" Rosemarie made a dismissive snort. "Wish I would have seen that earlier. It would have saved me a world of time."

The statement sounded out of place for a desperate woman who was so amenable and genial yesterday. Donna's head cleared the steps, and she could see both women standing and staring at each other. They both had hands on their hips and heads at an angle. It made her think of warring chickens. Her mother would not appreciate the comparison. Even though Cecilia was no spring chicken—oops, chicken analogy again—her money would be on her mother for her decades of experience and the ability to outmaneuver most others.

She'd always prided herself as a child when she outsmarted her mother because almost no one could mislead her parent. In the end, maybe she hadn't fooled her mother at all. It could have been the perceived infraction wasn't bad enough for the punishment or her mother was too tired to deal with it.

Rosemarie spotted Donna, first. "Oh look! My boss is here."

"I see." Cecilia nodded. "Anything you want to tell your newest hire?"

"Problems?" Donna managed a feigned curious tone as if she hadn't just listened to the entire conversation.

"This woman—" Rosemarie pointed to Cecilia.

Before she could go any further, Donna felt the need to say,

"You mean my mother?"

She wasn't sure who Rosemarie thought Cecilia was. A random guest who decided to criticize the housekeeping staff maybe.

"Oh," Rosemarie mumbled and deflated the tiniest little bit. "Never mind."

It was obvious she needed to make some things clear before she headed off on her fact-finding mission. She smiled at both of them but made eye contact with her mother, who would corner her and tell her exactly what she thought of Rosemarie later.

"My mother, Cecilia, comes and helps with the inn from time to time. She's familiar with how I like everything done." Donna mentally added that her mother usually tended to do things *her* way, despite knowing the inn protocols because she thought her way was better. "She has been kind enough to offer her help while I'm gone."

Rosemarie's mouth dropped open. Possibly she realized how much she resembled a beached fish and snapped her lips together. "Where are you going?" She cut her eyes to Cecilia. "When will you be back?"

They were odd questions to be asking an employer. The woman shifted her feet as she waited for an answer. Was she apprehensive, fearing that Cecilia would be a hard taskmaster? Personally, Donna felt her mother was less demanding, but it looked like the two got off to a bad start.

"No worries," Donna said, taking a line from a reggae song that blasted from the speakers of various beach businesses. Tourists didn't want to think about trouble back home. "I'll be back before supper. I'm sure my mother can find something to eat for lunch. She's been cooking for half a century."

"Donna!" her mother exclaimed in an irritated tone at what she considered a poke at her age. Despite having a daughter in her fifties, Cecilia liked to pretend she wasn't a day over sixty.

"Gotta go." She was ready to turn but felt obliged to soften the blow about her mother cooking for half a century, which was a lie because her mother hated cooking and got out of it as much as she could. At best, she could have cooked for possibly a decade. "Love you."

She was addressing her mother but she didn't know if Rosemarie understood this. She might think she was a very weird boss indeed. "I meant my mother. I love her."

Before she could explain more, Cecilia made a shooing gesture with her hand and said, "Go. I have it all under control."

Chapter Eighteen

DONNA BLEW OUT an audible breath as the car in front of her slowed. At this close angle, it was easy to see the driver was peering at something in her hand, then up at the street sign. The license plate announced the driver was from *The Land of Lincoln,* which meant not a local. *Be patient.* Her fingers inched closer to the horn, but she drew them back. Legacy needed the business the out-of-towners provided. The inn needed the business. So far, it had been a hard sell to convince locals that staying at the inn in the town where they already lived would make for a special weekend. Most would rather stay at home with their widescreen television and where the pizza guy knew their address. Tourists she could accept with open arms. It was the congestion they caused on the narrow roads she could do without.

She kept pace with the looker since she couldn't do much else with traffic zooming by on her left side. While she might be tempted to pass if there wasn't traffic there, she knew better with a double solid yellow line. Whenever she even thought about a traffic infraction, Legacy's finest showed up. Most of the time, they simply told Mark as if she were a wayward teen he needed to school in the art of driving. The possibility of that happening again made her watch her speed, kept her from any rolling stops no matter what, and made her very leery of passing anyone on a solid line road no matter the time of day or traffic situation. If nothing else, it gave her time to think.

The gull cries drifted into her open window along with the ocean breeze. In the distance, she could hear some shouts and whoops. Apparently, someone just won their heat. It was a great day for a race with a cloudless blue sky stretching forever. With any luck, it would be a great day to uncover some clues the police missed or even better, finding the missing millionaire. Who knows? He could be watching the race in disguise, wanting to see the reaction his disappearance caused. It would be a gutsy and stupid move, but more than one person had tried a similar stunt.

The *chuff-chuff* of a helicopter caused her to lean forward to peer out her windshield to locate the source, without luck. She hoped it was heading to the coast to catch the race as opposed to being a police copter. There would be a good chance of Mark riding along to keep a bird's eye view of the ransom drop. He'd recognize her car and wonder what she was up to. It wouldn't take any major deductive skills to realize she was quite a way from her usual haunts and the inn. He'd also know she hadn't mentioned going anywhere.

Fortunately, the car in front of her found its address and turned off. Hallelujah! Donna tapped the gas but kept the speed at just four miles over the limit. If she didn't have to resort to driving out to Leroy's Good Enough Tackle and Bait shop for a hunting dog, she would be on the edge of the town limits. Her last encounter with a retired bloodhound was lively. Who knew the dog could be so strong and out of control when on the trail of its quarry? She hadn't. There was a good chance Mark had told the owner never to let her borrow the dog again. Even if he hadn't, she decided to go with a smaller, easier to handle dog, which explained the drive.

Between Mark and her, there wasn't a ton of leisure time, but every now and then they squeezed out a day or two. Her beloved had accompanied her to various real estate auctions for inn supplies and even agreed to stay in a bed and breakfast to check out the competition. It was only fair to do something he liked, which was fishing. Besides a coastline, Legacy had a river and a few oversized stocked ponds euphemistically called *lakes*. That's how she ended up meeting Leroy and his beagle, Peanut.

At the time, Donna had no great plans to borrow the dog, but she had stored away the owner's bragging about his pet's tracking skills. Beagles were known for their keen sense of smell. They can remember fifty different scents, and their sense of smell was forty-five times better than a human's. A few could even sniff out cancer. With their short legs allowing them to be close to the ground, they didn't have to stop and regain a scent as the bigger dogs do. Their noses are so sensitive they're being used now to sniff out bed bugs. While she didn't think J.D. smelt anything like a bedbug, she only hoped Peanut could pick up a scent from the tie.

While calling up and offering the man money to borrow his dog was a long shot, she did it anyway. While she didn't exactly say the dog was for police purposes, there could have been an implication that it was official business. You'd think a local would offer the dog free, but the tackle and bait shop could be one of the businesses that didn't profit from the regatta. Fifty dollars covered her rental for the first couple of hours, then it went up. How long could it take to sniff a boat? As far as she could tell, the sailing yachts weren't that large. Certainly not big enough to be worthy of the name *yacht*. The term brought to mind luxurious crafts, complete with white-coated waiters serving champagne to glamorous women in slinky dresses and skyscraper heels, standing next to their much older husbands.

Technically, the definition of a yacht was twenty-three meters, which was about the length of a sixty-foot mobile home. Although there were a few locals that could float a mobile home, she'd doubt they'd call it a yacht.

A series of handmade signs with suspect spelling announced the upcoming bait shop. *Better slow your hosses down. If'n you want bait + beer. Almost there. Your here!* Donna winced at the last sign's poor grammar.

The tires grumbled as Donna pulled into the gravel parking lot. A rust-decorated pickup featured a magnetic sign, decorated with a happy fish with a fin wrapped around a can. As she walked closer, she noticed someone had managed to work in the word *beer* on the can as if there were any doubts about what fish preferred to drink. A speech bubble over the fish read, "Fish use Pretty Good Tackle and Bait Shop."

Really? Donna shook her head. There was so much wrong with the sign besides a beer-swilling fish. First of all, it was way too hard to see from far away. If a person was already at the bait shop, they were probably going to buy bait anyhow. Oh well, Leroy was trusting enough to let her borrow his trusted canine companion. No reason to point out that fish would not recommend any bait or tackle shop.

Inside the shop, Zydeco music was playing, and a dog howled along with it. A man in bibbed overalls with long, graying hair pulled into a ponytail had his back to her and was arranging lures on metal pegs.

"Excuse me," Donna said. Neither the dog nor the man responded. Of course not. How could they hear with the music blasting? She raised her voice. "Pardon me! I came about the dog?" Still nothing. Even though she'd been taught to respect personal boundaries and wished her guests would do likewise, she stepped behind the counter and clicked off the radio. The dog shot her an indignant glance, then let out a long howl, which caused the man to spin around and pull out his earbuds. "Why'd ya shut off the music?"

Donna put one hand on her hip and raised an eyebrow. "You had earbuds in. How could you be listening?"

The man shot her a disbelieving look. "The music is for Peanut. He enjoys listening to the music of his homeland."

"Okay." She nodded. It was obvious the dog was jamming. It made her wonder if her own puggle had musical preferences. "I'm Donna. I called about the dog. Remember?"

"Yep." He gave a short nod. "Bring the money?"

"I did." She glanced over at the dog, who stopped howling and now gave a few slow wags of his tail. It was weird that the man didn't want to give her a list of how to take care of his pet. Money appeared to be the bottom line for Leroy. "Any special instructions?"

"Hmm…" Leroy's brow furrowed as he considered the matter. "You can feed and water him. Especially water him with the weather being what it is."

"Okay, I'll plan on it." She didn't expect to keep the dog long enough to feed him. All the same, she should know what he ate. "Any special dog food brand?"

"Nah," Leroy wrinkled his nose. "He'll eat what you eat. Don't go giving him any rich desserts, though. I'm trying to thin him down for hunting season. He can stand to lose a pound or two." With that pronouncement, he gave Donna the once over, which ruffled her feathers and caused her to suck in her stomach.

Overall, she considered herself in pretty good shape for her age. Sure, she did taste more than a few delicious desserts that she served her guests. What kind of cook would she be if she didn't taste her own food? "Anything else?"

"He's not a fan of stewed okra or tomatoes."

"Tomatoes," she echoed the word. Not that she had any intention of feeding the dog tomatoes.

"Just the stewed kind. He's right fond of spaghetti sauce and spaghetti."

"Good to know." Donna pulled her wallet out of her purse and scanned the room for a clock. She found an old school clock that had seen better days. "Let's start the time at eleven."

Leroy turned to peer at the clock. "It's two minutes to eleven. Let's start it at two minutes to eleven."

Oh, he was going to be like that, huh? Donna plucked the fifty dollars out of her wallet and waved it. "I can wait until eleven. It will be easier to remember eleven."

Leroy grumbled something under his breath and took the fifty dollars on his way to get the dog. He attached a leash to the aging beagle, who started wagging his tail harder. He handed the leash to Donna. "I expect my Peanut to be returned in the same condition. Once you go over your time, it's seventy-five dollars an hour. Cash only."

On the phone, they had agreed on fifty dollars for two hours. She was certain she could get done what she needed in two hours. Still, what if she didn't? Costs were stacking up on her deductive mission. "You jumped up the price fast."

"A man needs his dog." He managed a sage nod and folded his arms as if that was the end of the matter.

No use arguing about it. She needed to be quick about it. "Anything else I need to know?"

Leroy had put his earbuds in and turned back to sorting inventory. She'd take that as a *no*. When she opened the door, Peanut shot out, giving her arm a good yank. Donna yanked back, glad she had a tight hold on the leash. It wouldn't have killed the man to mention the beagle wasn't leash trained.

Despite finding many great scents on the ground that Peanut wanted to follow, Donna managed to herd him into the backseat. Once inside the car, she started it and turned on the police scanner. Mark wasn't a fan of her having one, afraid it would make her worry unduly. Secretly, he probably worried she'd try to solve every crime she heard going down in the area. Her hubby finally consented when she pointed out they often used her car when riding together. This way he could keep track of any criminal activity in Legacy, but so could Donna.

There was static, then she heard her hubby's voice. "Two suspects headed for the ransom drop."

It sounded like there might not be any need for Peanut's clue sniffing service, but just to be sure, Donna decided to try a little drive-by. The junior high was about twenty minutes away. By the time she got there, it would all be over but the shouting. She'd pick up a box of donuts on her way. It might be stereotypical, but she'd never witnessed the officers pass on fresh, bakery donuts, which would add another ten minutes to her commute. With any luck, everyone would still be at the school. Peanut gave a sharp bark.

"No donuts for you." She felt bad for the dog. "I know. Diets are hard."

Chapter Nineteen

THE WARM, SWEET aroma of yeast donuts filled the car, making Donna salivate a tiny bit. No donuts for her. She reminded herself of the inference that someone ate too many yummy desserts. Maybe she had. In a way, it was her job to sample the food. No one ever trusted a skinny cook. Her left hand gripped the steering wheel while her right hand inched its way toward a donut. Rather like something from a Poe story or those old black-and-white movies, her hand was on a mission while the rest of the body was clueless. The difference was Donna knew exactly what her hand was up to.

There was an occasional crackle from the police scanner, but no actual words. For security, they'd switched to a different frequency—one that wasn't being monitored by the locals. Thank goodness Donna had a reason for showing up. Normally there would be some side looks that she happened to know where the ransom drop was, but the note had been taped to her inn door. If anyone complained, she'd point out she was savvy enough not to pick it up with her fingers.

Even though her radio was turned down to hear the scanner, her cell phone still rang through on it. The number displayed on the small screen that served as a backup camera and a GPS. It was her mother. Her hand gave up its progress toward the donut box to push the *Accept* button. It had only been thirty minutes since Donna left. All she asked her mother to do was answer any questions the guests might have and make sure the rooms were clean. What could have happened?

"Hello, Mother."

"Glad I caught you." Her mother spoke in a rushed tone.

"Is anything wrong?"

"Technically no, but I have a feeling," her mother reported.

Not her, too. Wasn't it enough to have Thelma drop by and predict imminent danger for Donna? Even though she reassured herself that Thelma's last pronouncement hadn't panned out, it was still unnerving. "I'm fine, by the way. I just stopped to get some donuts for the officers."

"Oooh, good move. They'll love it." Cecilia exhaled as if she had been holding her breath. "I'll feel better having you surrounded by our boys in blue."

No need to mention that she'd only be there long enough to see if her field trip with Peanut was a go or a no-go. Either way, Leroy would not be giving her any money back. That much she could guarantee without any psychic skills. Her mother never claimed any ESP abilities, but when she had a *feeling*, something usually happened. Unfortunately, it was never great, such as winning the lottery. One time her brother broke his leg. Another was the first and only car wreck Donna ever had, and it was a doozy. The last time before today was when her father had his fatal heart attack. Maybe she'd do well to listen to her mother. "What's your feeling?"

"It was nothing, I guess. Probably brought on by Rosemarie. That woman is difficult. She won't even gossip about her family."

This is why her mother called her? "She said plenty to me. It's not a good situation, which means she's embarrassed by it. Doesn't want to tell everyone. Why does it matter?"

Silence made Donna wonder if they were disconnected. Then

her mother said in a dismissive manner, "Oh, never mind. I have no doubt both you and Mark checked out her references."

That's what any thinking person would do. She'd meant to but felt, after the sob story, that Rosemarie wouldn't have any pertinent ones. The woman was anxious because her brother had badmouthed her around. "Yeah," she agreed. "That's the most basic thing to do."

She made a mental note to do so when she got back. Things had been so hectic lately. Maybe she could call Maria up, and she could do an online search of the public records. If nothing else, it let you know if someone had been arrested or failed to pay their property taxes.

"Call me a worry wart. See ya, sweetie."

"Love you." Donna spoke the words, almost certain her mother had already hung up. What was it with everyone hanging up on her lately?

Traffic became more problematic the closer she came to the middle school. Before she could make it to the three-story brick building that was as old or older than Donna, there was a police barricade. *Great.* She should have known she just couldn't drive up to the school when something was going down.

Time to use her connections and charm. It would be up to her marital status to Legacy's top-performing veteran detective to open the proverbial door since her charm was in limited supply. Unlike most Southern women, she never learned the gentle art of flirting and promising nothing. Her window slid down as she approached a uniformed officer.

He leaned into the open window. "Ma'am, this area is closed to the public. You need to turn around and pick another route."

She forced her lips into a wide smile, then chuckled. "I'm no *ma'am.* I mean, I'm Donna Tabor. Mark Tabor's wife. Surely you've heard of me?"

"I have," the officer acknowledged with something akin to amusement in his eyes. He coughed, cleared his throat, and said, "What can I do for you, Mrs. Tabor?"

"Oh," she gestured airily back to the donut box. "I brought some treats for our hard-working men and women in blue."

"You mean the box your dog is tearing into?"

For a second, she wondered what Jasper had to do with it. There was the sound of tearing cardboard, which had Donna turning in time to push Peanut back into the back seat. "Stop that! You're on a diet."

He'd taken advantage of her inattention to stick his head between the seats in order to grab a bakery goodie. Donna flipped the box open, revealing three dozen untouched donuts, no thanks to Peanut. She picked up a napkin from the seat and used it to extract a donut. "Here ya go, Officer." She handed over the sweet. "Maybe you could call someone to take the donuts to the officers. If this is a good time?" She hoped the casual delivery inquiry might net her the needed information.

The officer, whose name tag read *Reasor*, spoke into his shoulder radio. "Detective Tabor's wife is at the roadblock in front of the school."

Donna winced. She didn't need Mark to trot out to see her. Not only would she be interrupting whatever was happening, but he'd also see through her donut ploy. Worse, he might think something horrible had happened, such as the inn burning to the ground. There was a crackle from the radio and something unintelligible. Reasor nodded as if whoever he was talking to could see him. "He's on his way."

Exactly what she didn't want. Any other wife would be pleased with such a courtesy. "Ah, thank you, Officer. That was very kind. Another donut?"

"Oh, no. I want to save some for the others." He used his free hand to point to the curb. "You might want to move your car over there. Once we open the roadblock, we'll have vehicles coming out this way."

"Okay," she readily offered as she processed the information, he had so artlessly given her. There were several officers on duty. Maybe he was afraid her three dozen donuts wouldn't be enough. Vehicles were also in play, which made her wonder what they were. Usually, parking a bunch of squad cars around a drop site served as a dead giveaway. Even though Donna considered leaving for a second, she knew such behavior wouldn't reflect well on Mark or her, especially since she'd be taking the offered donuts with her. Staying meant the clock was ticking on her fifty dollars. Every minute was a little bit closer to being a very expensive beagle rental.

Another officer showed up and helped Reasor remove the barrier. There was a rumble of heavy vehicles. Donna turned, expecting a fire engine or maybe an ambulance, but instead saw a trio of yellow school buses. Very clever. Buses would be expected at school and could hide a number of officers, too. Through the last bus windows, she saw a number of SWAT-suited officers decked out in their black clothing. Even though the bus obscured most of their bodies, she knew they'd donned bulletproof vests and helmets that gave them a sci-fi robot look when worn.

There was no mention of gunfire on the scanner, which meant it must have gone according to plan without a shot exchanged. On the plus side, her husband was safe. She should be happy. J.D. Sizemore would be back in the headlines again, although he hadn't really left them. Only this time it would be for something more than just disappearing.

Behind the buses, a plain beige sedan followed. Most people wouldn't look twice at it, but its very plainness shouted *undercover cop car* to her. It wasn't plastered with stick people, various sports emblems, or decals announcing how far the driver had run or favorite vacation spots. Most cars served as billboards for the driver's interests and family status. Back to the sedan, there was a metal grid between the officers in the front seat and some very morose-looking teen boys in the back. Was that who she thought it was? She blinked. Since the first school bus stopped, everyone had to, and it gave Donna a chance to examine the miscreants in the car. They were kids from the neighborhood. Donnie, whom the parents had christened Donald William Treadwell III, and his partner in crime, Teddy, who happened to be a 3rd, also.

Whatever they were accused of, Donna was fairly certain they were guilty. One time, she caught them throwing lit firecrackers in her yard to scare Jasper. After that experience, her pup had no love for the two. The memory of Jasper running to the gate and barking madly came to mind as she nabbed a donut, tore it in two, and offered half to Peanut.

"I should have listened to my dog. He knew all along."

The vehicles started moving again at the same time as her passenger door opened. Her husband, Mark, bent to address her and noticed the box. "Beulah's donuts. Good deal. I assume you brought this for Legacy's Finest."

"Of course."

Her hubby reached into the car and picked up the box. "I'm sure this had nothing to do with your checking out the kidnappers."

Initially, she planned on denial, but the truth always worked better. "I was curious."

"Dead end." He shook his head. "Back to the drawing board, I'm afraid."

"I saw Donnie and Teddy in the back of that car."

Mark bit into a donut and nodded as he chewed. Finally, he swallowed. "Those two are a nuisance. We just wasted manpower chasing around after them. They're not kidnappers, but a couple of boneheads." He gestured with his donut. "You were right. They did mention the movie. Thought it was an easy way to score some money."

"Why they need money, considering who their parents are, surprises me. It could have been the thrill to see if they could get away with it."

"Possibly," Mark agreed. "Did you get any coffee to wash the donuts down?"

Donna reached over to the passenger floor and pulled up a heavy sack. "I had my doubts about doing so but knew you drink that sludge that passes for coffee at the station. That has to be even worse for your ulcer."

"True," he agreed with a grin. He popped the rest of the donut in his mouth and took the proffered sack. Peanut chose that moment to stick his head up and barked.

Good Lord! She had almost got away without too many questions. "You better get those donuts to the station while they are still fresh."

"What's with the beagle?" Mark took a step back as Donna reached across the seat to close the door.

"I'm dog sitting. I'll explain it to you when you get home." She slammed the door shut, but on second thought, powered the window down just in time to hear her hubby say,

"Why do I think I'm not going to like your explanation?" His brows beetled together as he considered the matter.

Donna blew him a kiss before she roared off.

Chapter Twenty

WAVES ROCKED THE *Foam Empress* as she sat at anchor in the harbor. The turquoise-colored craft had an image of a woman with hard eyes, tight lips, and a crown on her head painted on its side. Donna would have taken J.D. Sizemore for the type who would have had an elaborate figurehead on the prow of his ship—some young buxom beauty with flowing hair who would be the eyes of the ship. Curious, she'd researched the subject and discovered that in the early days, ships were viewed as living things that needed eyes to explore the seas. The figureheads served as both religious protection from unknown powers that might assail them and also as a guardian.

The early ships had figureheads that were fearsome animals, such as boars, snakes or dragons, to intimidate any other ships, their inhabitants, and the inhabitants' guardian spirits. Along the way, England created beautiful women as figureheads, usually barebreasted. Donna wrinkled her nose at the thought and muttered, "Typical."

The women represented whatever name the ship bore, which was bound to be feminine. Men had a tendency to call both boats and cars *she*. Freud would have a heyday with that. Donna felt it was probably one of the few times a man could assert dominance over a woman. The idea made her chuckle and had the beagle she was leading gaze up at her.

A few curious onlookers had made the trip down to the pier to see and possibly take a selfie of themselves with the *Empress*. As they passed Donna and her dog-for-the-day, a few nodded. All the crowd saw was a middle-aged woman walking a dog. Little did they know one of the town's greatest crime solvers walked among them.

Peanut was quite a change from the bloodhound she'd borrowed for a previous case. That dog almost tore her arm out of her socket when he hit the scent. There might be white on Peanut's muzzle, but he was still a trained hunting dog.

She needed to be quick. Leroy warned her if she were a minute late, the fee would be tripled. In her pocket was the silk Armani tie Tabitha had given her. The cast-off girl friend had stolen back her gift when she found out that her time as celebrated arm candy was up. It didn't necessarily mean the man ever wore it, although Tabitha insisted it had been used.

A couple of policemen had been stationed by the *Empress* to keep the nosy at a distance. She eyed the young officers, recognizing one. Jackson was a newer officer who came from Ashville. Most of Legacy's Finest were born in Legacy or, at the very least, were raised there. Those who came from bigger cities often regarded the place as an ignorant backwater town without basic forensic tools. The basic tools part was true, which is why she borrowed Peanut. The other officers took affront at the description.

Mark decided to take Jackson under his wing when the young man applied to the force to be closer to his girlfriend, who was a Legacy native. A man who didn't insist his lady love had to move to *his* city was all right in her book. Jackson was a bonus. A plan developed as she walked, but she'd only have seconds to enact it. It was up to her to solve the crime, and save the reputation of her town and its police force. The commissioner wanted to call the FBI in—an admission that their police couldn't get the job done, as far as she was concerned.

She bent down under the guise of petting Peanut but had the tie in her hand. The fabric reeked of aftershave, affirming that it had been worn. The dog sniffed it, backed up a little, and panted. It was probably trying to draw in fresh air.

"Peanut, go, find."

There was a spark in the beagle's eyes, and then he put his head down and begin to sniff. Donna was fairly sure there would be no scent of Sizemore on the pier, but she could be wrong. It had happened on rare occasions. She gently guided the dog toward the boat and waved at Jackson. "How's it going?"

"It's going," Jackson acknowledged.

The other officer nodded in her direction. He said something to Jackson, and then jogged past Donna. As she drew closer, Jackson pointed to Peanut, who was doing a thorough sweep of the wooden pier as far as his long leash would permit. Her thumb rested on the button that released the full length of the leash, all twelve feet. Her hope was that Peanut would scent Sizemore on the gangway and scramble aboard the boat.

As she drew closer to Jackson, she smiled. "Looks to me like you drew the pick of the duties."

"Ha!" He forced out the laugh. "I'd rather be out searching as opposed to guarding the boat. I understand some of the other sailors would like a peek at it. There's probably an enterprising thief who could sail it, too. At this point, I discourage rubbernecking and listen to Ross whine about how I'm wasting his time when he could actually be at the regatta. It's not like I assigned him this duty. Our shift ends in about ten minutes, anyhow. That's why I told Ross to go on ahead." Jackson grimaced. "Forget I said anything. Please don't say anything to your husband. He put his neck out recommending me for a promotion. I don't want him to think I'm not appreciative or doing my job."

Donna jiggled the leash, trying to get Peanut's attention. He was spending too much sniff time on a discarded fast-food wrapper. A dog-for-hire didn't come with any guarantees. Old Peanut might need to be pushed in the right direction. The extension leash worked both ways. She wiggled it, then retracted it, pulling the beagle in, a bit like landing a fish. When she had the dog close enough, she chose to answer Jackson. "Mark knows you're grateful. He certainly knows you're a hard worker. He told me he wished there were more like you on the force."

Actually, Mark had not, since he tried to talk about work as little as possible when he finally arrived home. Still, if her hubby was more of a chatterbox, he might have said something like that.

The officer's gaze dropped to the ground. "That's nice of you to say."

It was rather nice, she concurred, but she needed the man looking up to allow her to do her magic with Peanut. Most men in love enjoyed discussing their beloved. "How's your girl liking your living so close by?"

Jackson's face lit up, and he launched into talking about a small cottage that was up for sale. It would be perfect for newlyweds. As the man described the fixer-upper, Donna tried to bump Peanut in the right direction. She even went so far as to think the word *gangway*, but she wasn't sure if the dog was familiar with the term. He spent his time working at a bait shop, but he struck her like a dog who didn't pay close attention.

Peanut sat beside her and panted. At her first leg bump, the dog moved a couple of inches and sat down again. That was a total fail.

Donna kept nodding at Jackson as he talked about the stove needing to be replaced.

"Do you think I should do this on my own or ask Allyson about it?"

This was one she could answer, not even knowing the female. "You definitely need to ask her. You don't want to go to all this work and find out she'd rather have done it differently. Remember, it's not a house, it's a home." She made a sweeping gesture on the last word, hoping it would hide her sidestep to get closer to the dog.

Just when she'd almost given up all hope of getting the beagle to move at all, a tiger-striped cat strolled down the pier, heading their way. His tail was in the air, as was his nose. It was obvious they were in his territory. He must not have seen Peanut or considered the dog unworthy of concern. When the feline was about five feet from them, Peanut erupted into frenzied barking that caused the cool and collected cat to pause, then veer suddenly onto the *Foam Empress's* gangway. Peanut gave a sharp yank and chased after the cat. For a half-second, Donna tried to pull the dog back, then dropped the leash, realizing this was the opportunity she wanted.

"Oh my!" Donna pressed her hands to her cheeks the way she had seen actresses demonstrate distress. "He's my friend's dog. I need to get him before he gets hurt."

"Well, um, Mrs. Taber, I really should be doing that." Jackson was quick to offer.

"No problem," Donna said as she stepped onto the gangway. "You need to man your post and keep folks away from the boat. I'll just pop in, grab the dog, and be back in a jiffy."

Jackson started after her, but a strolling couple asked him to take their photo, which he was obliged to do to preserve Legacy's slogan, *The Welcoming City*. Donna took advantage of the officer's momentary inattention. Even though she moved fast, it was hard not to notice the two big outboard motors and all the gadgetry near the captain's wheel. It didn't take a boat expert to realize major money had been spent on the craft.

No sign of her rented dog or the cat, which meant they were probably below. Donna stepped carefully down the stairs that led to quite a stylish little cabin with a working kitchen, table, and wraparound seats. Dampness still hung in the air. The cushioned seats were probably plumper than they were originally. Experimentally, she moved the toe of her shoe across the floor. It felt dry. At least part of the craft had recovered from its dip in the sea.

There was a grappling hook on the wall, probably used to fish out sailors who fell into the water. Despite its waterlogged state, the boat still felt luxurious. She doubted the other entrants in the race had such a nice craft.

Hissing, along with a canine whimper, let her know who was winning the battle. Donna passed a minuscule toilet, noting how clean it was as if no one had had the chance to dirty it up yet. Near the front of the boat was a queen-sized mattress perched on a platform and wedged in by walls. It was a little close-quarters for her taste. Right on top of the expensive comforter set was a cowering Peanut. "Oh, there you are."

She spoke the words in case anyone was listening. The striped menace paraded by with enough attitude for five felines. So far, she hadn't noticed anything unusual about the boat except it was unusually clean for a craft that recently had half a dozen men on it. It had foundered in the waves, possibly dumping all its trash.

Donna made a grab for Peanut, who jumped off the bed, exposing a wet spot. *Great.* The least she could do was try to blot up the spot. The acrid odor of dog urine made her crinkle her nose.

Underneath was another scent, one she recognized from her decades at the hospital.

Outside there was a splash and a scream. "Someone save her! She can't swim!"

Donna rushed to one of the tiny windows to see what was happening. A loud splash was heard, and then Officer Jackson surfaced in full uniform. *What in the world was going on?* His radio would short out in the water, and those things weren't cheap.

She needed to get topside immediately and call Mark to report her suspicions. It was hard to know what to do first. With no time to blot the comforter, Donna had Peanut tucked under one arm, not willing to take a chance on the pooch escaping.

Footsteps sounded on the galley steps. Donna turned slowly, not sure who it could be. Her breath caught as she contemplated who it *might* be. There was no real place to hide, especially with a canine who was even now whimpering to get down. When she saw who it was, her breath released in a whoosh. "Thank goodness it's you!"

Chapter Twenty-One

C YNTHIA, THE SOFTER, quieter part of her New England visitors, stood on the interior steps of the *Foam Empress*. She pressed a hand to her heart as she swept an appreciative gaze over the interior. "It's nice. Very nice. Everything I thought it would be."

The appearance of her guest and not a criminal bent on felonious activity had Donna loosening her hold on Peanut, who wriggled to the floor. The beagle ran back to the bed, scratching at the edge of it, and whimpering. While the canine's behavior was odd, Cynthia's behavior was a trifle more peculiar. If there was one New Englander, there was bound to be the other. Personally, she could do without another brush with the acerbic Eugenia. "Ah, where's your cousin?"

"Which one?" Cynthia inquired with a slight smile.

Oh, right, they came down to watch another cousin race. "Eugenia."

The woman's shoulders went up in a shrug. "Hard to say. She goes where she wants to go. We were on the beach and suddenly she wasn't with me." Cynthia pressed her fingers together, then pulled them apart fast, indicating the vanishing companion.

It was hard to believe Eugenia would disappear without an explanation or a demand to accompany her. Outside of the pier, there really wasn't all that much to see. The shops gathered around the pier were only big enough for the seller and supplies inside. Unless Eugenia took over the running of the Hot Dog Stop or the Ice

Cream Wagon, she should be easily visible. Something wasn't right. She could see a local, aggravated enough with Eugenia's superior attitude, wanting to push her into the water, which reminded her of the earlier splash. Maybe it had been her mouthy guest who'd taken an impromptu swim.

Peanut, who had had enough of being ignored, started barking.

"Will you shut that mutt up!" Cynthia uncharacteristically bellowed, and then shot a quick glance over her shoulder.

No lightbulb needed to go on over Donna's head. The tone of the request didn't sound a bit like the mousy woman who checked in. Better yet, why was she here? Near the pocket bathroom was a pole with a hook on it used to rescue folks or possibly floating objects in the water. As weapons go, it was better than nothing. Not nearly as good as the handgun her hubby had gifted her with that she'd left in the car. Her reasoning had been she wouldn't need it, especially with two of Legacy's finest on duty. Too bad one had hightailed it to the Regatta. Still, Jackson should still be on duty. A scream should bring him running. The idea, while a possibility, made her cringe. That would make her no better than the various movie females who were always being rescued by their male co-stars.

Donna inhaled, ready to let loose a yell when she realized that if Jackson was on duty, Cynthia wouldn't have been allowed on the yacht. Her hand went to the back of her neck as she glanced at the exit Cynthia was blocking. Despite being a mere eight giant steps away, it might as well be a mile. The hook was her best option when it came to impromptu weapons.

All she had to do was work her way the few feet to grab it. It would be best to act as if she had no clue what was happening.

"Nice day out there. I bet the two of you wanted to see the yachts up close."

"Yes." Cynthia pushed out the words through gritted teeth and placed her hand behind her back. "Plenty of folks out. I wouldn't be surprised if someone stumbled across J.D.'s body today."

Even though the word *dead* wasn't said, it was implied. Donna didn't want to speculate on how she knew or even if she was right.

"Ah," she said the word while hoping that her excellent, detective husband would be suspicious of her driving around with a strange dog. Would he suspect she was here?

Even though Donna had been in tight situations before, this one was tricky. Cynthia blocked her exit. The woman pulled her hand from behind her back, complete with a Magnum pistol that was pointed straight at Donna. Not good. Things just became a little trickier.

Donna gulped hard. "I can leave now. All you had to do was ask."

Cynthia gave a mirthless chuckle. "I imagine you'd like that. Go run and tell the nearest policeman there's a crazy Yankee with a gun. I'll let you go, *eventually*. First, you need to shut up your dog, or I'll shoot it," she declared, waving the pistol in the canine's direction. It had an extra inch to the nozzle—a silencer.

Peanut wasn't her dog, but Donna still wouldn't stand for anything to happen to the annoying hound on her account. She bent over, catching the dog by the collar, petting it and hoping it had some training. Although their time together had been nada, she made a fuss over petting and shushing it, then pointed to the entrance that Cynthia had moved about a foot from. "Go! Now!"

Peanut rushed for Cynthia, who gave a quick step to the right, opening up the escape route. The beagle bounded up the stairs with his white tipped tail disappearing through the opening. Since Donna was no closer to the grappling hook, she reached back for the dog-urine-soaked coverlet and swung it at Cynthia. The acrid odor of gunpowder and the sensation of a bullet going over her shoulder stopped Donna's attack for a moment, but not Cynthia, who flailed and cursed under the coverlet. Even though it was taking a chance, Donna tackled the blanket-draped woman, expecting a bullet to penetrate the expensive fabric and enter her own skin.

The pistol skidded across the floor and had both Donna and Cynthia scrambling for it. Donna lunged for the weapon, her fingers only inches away when Cynthia, being closer, grabbed it first. They were two middle-aged women, prone on the floor of a rocking boat, tangled in a coverlet. Knowing the woman could not miss at this distance, Donna grabbed the edge of the coverlet and jerked hard, which threw the woman off-balance, causing the shot to go into the ceiling.

There was the sound of baying, then a scrabbling of dog nails above that caused both women to glance at the galley entrance. Donna hoped it was Peanut, returning with the cavalry. Taking advantage of the woman's inattention, she lurched to her knees, grabbed for the gun, and busted Cynthia in the face. Cynthia refused to give up the gun. Right hand still gripping tight, Cynthia slapped at Donna with her free hand.

A single bark announced Peanut's entrance as he jumped from the stairs, teeth bared. From her angle, Donna watched as Peanut clamped down on Cynthia's right arm. The gun tumbled to the floor. Donna dived for it and rolled, her hands wrapping around it.

Cursing, Cynthia tried to shake the dog free. "Get your stupid dog off me! It's ruining everything. This is *my* racing yacht! I created it."

There was the sound of running footsteps and then a call Donna was never so glad to hear: "Freeze! Police!"

Mark was the first one down the steps, followed by a dripping Officer Jackson. Peanut may have decided to let the police take over or maybe he was tired of being swung around. All it took was Mark saying *release* in a gruff tone for the dog to do so. Sirens sounded in the distance as Mark cuffed Cynthia, who was far from cooperative.

As Mark's arms closed around Donna and Jackson marched Cynthia up the stairs, she continued to yell. "You got nothing on me! I'm going to file for false arrest! Assault! The dog attacked me! It should be put down."

The sound of other officers above decks meant Jackson had backup. Sure, Jackson would need the help, Donna released a breath. A memory of someone yelling *she can't swim* came to mind as she settled into her husband's welcome embrace. "Did Jackson save the drowning victim?"

"Doll. It was a doll someone threw into the water and then yelled about it drowning. Of course, Jackson went after it thinking it was a baby. It's what I would have done."

"I know," Donna agreed, enjoying the quiet moment before all the questions began, such as *what did she think she was doing*? A whimper sounded, proving that Peanut was not a big fan of quiet moments. He was back at the bed, scratching.

As a hunting dog, he might not be the best, but he was an excellent guard dog. In the end, she knew she'd be paying a lot more than the fifty dollars she'd already given Leroy.

Underneath the ear pressed to her husband's chest, she heard his voice rumble. "Would you look at that!"

"What?" Donna pulled out of the embrace to see what interested her husband. Underneath the queen size mattress, a slick white surface peeked out. It definitely wasn't a box spring. As she drew closer, she noticed a low hum.

"Don't touch anything!" her husband warned.

Did he seriously think she was a novice? "Yes, I know. It looks like an appliance."

"Could be," Mark commented, and then turned and grabbed the grappling hook. He used it to push the mattress onto the floor exposing an oversized freezer with a lock. "I'm betting we just found J.D."

"Yes. Cynthia did say it was her boat. She created it, which meant she knew about the freezer."

"Hmm…" Mark mused as he ran his hand over his chin. "It's all starting to fit. Looks like we might have more than trespassing and assault on your guest."

"Good." Donna was more than a little miffed she hadn't noticed anything awry with her dangerous guest, but then no one else appeared to have noticed, either. "Didn't the officers think it was weird to have a huge freezer on the *Foam Empress*?"

"Hard to say." Mark grimaced. "Many vessels like this have freezers to store their catch. I'm curious why no one opened it." He held up one finger. "Trust me, I'll find out why. Unfortunately, most of the new recruits don't expect murder around every corner like you do."

Chapter Twenty-Two

A SONG ABOUT a guy missing the girl he left behind played softly in the corner of the kitchen as Donna put supper together. That she could even hear it with her mother peppering her with questions from her perch on a kitchen stool amazed her.

"Did you actually see the body?"

"Well, no," Donna admitted. Seeing dead people wasn't on her preferred list of things to do. What she wanted was the challenge of tracking down the killer. "Mark assured me J.D.'s frozen remains were in the freezer. Because he was frozen, it stopped decomposition, which meant no smell, but it didn't fool Peanut. He knew."

"Glad you didn't tell me your plans." Her mother wrinkled her nose. "I'd have told you it was crazy to expect anything from that beagle. He's more of a sideshow than a working dog. Folks drop by the bait shop to listen to him howl to music. Once there, they feel obliged to buy something, even if it's only a soda or a moon pie."

Because her mother couldn't see her expression as she bent to lift the cast iron skillet and place it on the stove, Donna smirked. She had deliberately *not* mentioned where she was going. First, her mother would have wanted to help which would have consisted of telling her how to do things. Secondly, there'd be no one to supervise Rosemarie or attend to the guests. "Here, I thought Peanut was a guard dog the way he attacked Cynthia when he saw the gun in her hand."

Cecilia gasped and pressed her hand to her heart. "You know what this means?"

"I was in danger, and you're grateful I survived another murder case. My ability to solve crimes is second to none." She cleared her throat, knowing she was a bit overboard on the last comment. "Well, maybe only second to my beloved. That's what you were going to say."

"No." Her mother shook her head, but her eyes were still big. "Thelma was right. She said you were in danger, and you were."

The would-be psychic was actually right about something. It made Donna remember their first meeting with her pint-sized demolition crew. "The first time she came by she said murder was in the air or something like that, which I brushed off."

"Aha, she really is psychic. Anything else? Any other pronouncements?" Cecilia pointed to herself. "Any winning lottery numbers?"

The possibility made Donna chuckle as she walked to the island where a bag of potatoes, a bowl half-full of water, a couple of peelers, and paring knives rested. "Yeah. I imagine any psychic who had winning numbers would use them herself. Come to think of it, she came about her brother on the second visit. She told me he was being framed and asked me to locate the guilty party."

"Was he?" Cecilia asked and picked up a peeler when Donna ripped open the bag of potatoes.

The outcome could have been very different for Jimmy Bobby with a less astute detective on board. "Yeah, he was. Turns out the temp ad for someone to crew the *Foam Empress* was a setup. Cynthia had a partner in crime: her brother. My amazing husband had his eye on Clyde, who got hurt mysteriously before the *Foam Empress's* ill-fated trip. It didn't seem right to hire someone locally who knew nothing about the boat. I would have expected them to have some alternates waiting in the wings. Turns out, when Jimmy Bobby was questioned, he insisted the guy with the neck brace was there. No one else mentioned seeing him."

Donna sat with an audible sigh and picked up a potato and a peeler. Fried potatoes were on the menu, along with pan-fried pork chops. A far cry from the lean meat and raw vegetables Mark was supposed to eat. She figured food her hubby actually liked now and then wouldn't be a crime. Besides, it was a celebration dinner. They solved another murder together.

"So, what was the deal with the neck brace guy? Did he kill J.D.?"

Less than ten minutes ago, Mark had called to inform her the brother was quick to turn on his half-sister for a deal. Cynthia, who had no idea what was going down, was insisting the worst she did was trespass on a boat, where she was attacked by a rabid dog. "It depends on how you see it."

Donna started to peel a potato and managed to get it down to the dicing part before Cecilia burst out with, "Girl, I raised you better than that!"

"Yes, Mother. When Mark questioned folks on the beach, one dude with a neck brace made a point to explain he should have been on the boat, but due to an accident, he ended up watching the race from the beach or at least that is what he wanted Mark to think. Turns out this was one of those long deals that took months or even years to play out. Cynthia found out Clyde was working for J.D. While she knew Clyde existed, the two of them hadn't had much contact. Her much younger brother was part of her father's second family."

"How did she convince Clyde to do the deed?"

"Well," Donna drew out the word. "We may never know since

we currently only have Clyde's version of the story that paints himself as a victim. We have a frozen dead guy who's thawing on the medical examiner's table. I figure parts of the story could be confirmed, especially about being drugged."

Her mother gestured with her peeler. "Get on with the story. What's the brother's explanation?"

"Ah, that." Donna dropped diced potatoes into the waiting bowl of water. "He said that Cynthia contacted him, saying she wanted to get to know her father's other family, especially since he had passed on."

"He died," Cecilia interrupted.

"No, he apparently moved on to another wife. It gave the two of them a shared experience of being abandoned by their father. Every month or so, Cynthia would invite Clyde to a hearty dinner at a local restaurant she paid for. He assumed they were connecting, but she was actually grooming him. She probably decided he wasn't all that sharp and would be easy enough to convince to go along with her scheme."

"He said that! Goodness."

"The part about not being too sharp was my guess. Do you want to hear the rest?"

Her mother narrowed her eyes as she spoke. "You know I do. Why bother asking?"

"I need to get the potatoes fried along with the pork chops. I don't have time for you to keep interrupting me, or I'll never finish anything."

Her mother gave a short nod, possibly to prove she wasn't going to interrupt, which lasted less than two seconds. "Do you think fried pork chops and fried potatoes in the same meal is wise? Maybe you could fix eggs instead of pork chops. Less fat, you know."

It was her mother's nature to interrupt and insert her opinion. Why would she expect her to change? Her mother pantomimed zipping her lips. Donna decided to continue Clyde's confession because hearing it again allowed her to check for discrepancies. She couldn't really *not* tell her mother, anyway.

"This meeting for a meal went on for months. Cynthia didn't say much outside of asking Clyde questions and talking about sailing. They both had shared a father who taught them to sail. In their conversations, he may have mentioned how demanding J.D. was and at times rather clueless about the mechanics of his racing yachts, which would explain his need for a seasoned crew. It was then that Cynthia decided to mention that most of the designs for the yachts were hers. Early on, she and J.D. had a relationship that was a type of partnership. She drew up all these designs for various racing yachts but had no money to create them. Initially, Cynthia tried to find backers without luck.

"Somewhere along the line, Cynthia had J.D. write out a note that all of the designs were hers and he had nothing to do with them. Clyde said she kept the note as an insurance policy but decided to take out a life insurance policy on J.D. as a joke. It was for half a million, which meant Cynthia needed a real job, as opposed to creating yacht designs, to pay the premiums. The woman attended MIT, which meant she knew her stuff. Whatever the real job was took her away from J.D., who soon replaced her with a wealthy beauty who funded the first yacht of the Sizemore line. Cynthia tried to fight back, but it was assumed she was bitter because J.D. had dumped her."

"Ah, I can visualize it," Cecilia said. She diced a potato into the water. "I bet she even increased the payout on the insurance policy."

"Possibly. It would have taken another signature from J.D. to do that, but not all agents were that conscientious and let her take the papers home to be signed. While J.D. was gaining fame on the racing yacht circuit, he wouldn't have been that well known to the average person."

"How did they do the deed?"

Well, she hadn't expected her mother not to interrupt. While she was tempted not to say another word, she knew she'd go ahead and explain. Cecilia's need to interject her comments or questions was just as strong as Donna's need to tell the tale.

"Eventually, Cynthia convinced Clyde she was being robbed of the fame and money she should have as the boat designer. She even explained the little extras she had created for the *Foam Empress* to make it better, sleeker, and faster than the competition. Once Clyde was convinced that she'd designed the yachts, she told him J.D. wasn't just ripping off Cynthia, it was the both of them since they were natural sailors and J.D. was an imposter."

There was a splash as another diced potato went into the bowl. Her mother gave a dismissive sniff. "Enough with the motivation. How was J.D. killed?"

"The original plan was to push him overboard, but with all the publicity boats, someone would be sure to rescue him. Even his own crew might fish him out despite the abuse he heaped on them. Unlike other owners who praised their crew when winning, J.D. took all the credit, which burned because he wasn't a very good sailor."

A chime of her mother's phone sounded. Cecilia extracted her phone from her purse and glanced at the number. "Mercy, I can't believe it. Hello?"

Donna waited, listening to the one-sided conversation, wondering who it could be that her mother would take a call in the middle of her exciting dénouement of the crime.

"That would be wonderful," Cecilia cooed. "Donna would be okay with it."

The mention of her name made Donna doubly curious. "Okay with what?"

Her mother ignored her and continued to chat. "Perfect. We can't wait to see you. Yes, I know it's short notice, but we can make it happen. Bye, now."

Short notice. Donna had a feeling the *we* was more like a *she.* Donna would make it happen. What was her mother promising now? "Who was that?"

"Never mind. Finish your story. Sorry about the interruption, but I wasn't the one who called. Go on. They decided against drowning."

Ah, she was going to play that game. Well, Donna was strong. She wouldn't beg. "J.D. liked to drink—a lot. Cynthia showed up with a bottle of his favorite booze, willing to let bygones be bygones."

"Let me guess. It was drugged." Her mother commented.

"You got that right. It messed with his balance and vision. Clyde wasn't sure if Cynthia's plan was for J.D. to wreck his car on his way to the race, but a crew member picked him up at the hotel and drove him to the pier. Clyde made a big show of wishing everyone well with his neck brace on. He introduced Jimmy Bobby as his replacement, which probably baffled the crew. Why would you put a clueless new guy on the yacht during a competition? Most probably he got in the way and they worked around Jimmy Bobby. Anyhow, Clyde sneaked back on during the boarding and hid in a supply closet. When Mark questioned the crew the first time, one member insisted he saw Clyde on the boat as opposed to being onshore, which meant Clyde wasn't as sneaky as he thought. Besides, the boats aren't that large."

Cecilia pursed her lips before she spoke, "The tale was bound to unravel eventually. Surprised Jimmy Bobby didn't say anything about Clyde being on board."

"I'm not. Maybe the boy was rattled when picked up by police and questioned about J. D.'s disappearance. No matter." She exhaled audibly. "Unfortunately. The info didn't come soon enough to save Legacy's reputation as a great place to have a regatta. Anyhow, gullible Jimmy Bobby was brought in as the most likely suspect. Clyde managed to get the drugged J.D. downstairs on the pretext of telling him information about a spy on board. He hit the woozy J.D. on the head and locked him into the freezer. He insisted he didn't kill J.D. because he was alive when he put him in the freezer. He also added it was a mercy killing since J.D. had a fatal disease."

Cecilia stopped peeling and arched her eyebrows in inquiry.

Look at her resisting the desire to ask the obvious question. Donna took sympathy on her mother and answered the unvoiced question. "Cynthia supposedly told him a story about J.D. dying or Clyde made it up to sound less like a cold-blooded killer. Either way, he was supposed to get a cut from the profits from the Sizemore boat line."

"There's no reason to think Cynthia would inherit," her mother said and pressed her lips together, well aware she had broken her promise not to talk several times.

"I know that. Cynthia does, too. It appears Clyde is both dupe and killer in this murder. The yacht was using a motor to assist with maneuvers, especially turning. Clyde had given Jimmy Bobby a shirt and hat to wear that was different from the crew and attired himself in a similar outfit, thinking if anyone saw him they would think he was Jimmy Bobby, who he pushed overboard before dumping J.D. in a freezer, fouling the propellers with a metallic fishnet, and moving a couple of sails to capsize the yacht. By the time the crew realized what had happened, Clyde had jumped overboard. Of course, the crew must have thought he was Jimmy Bobby."

Her mother blinked a few times as if trying to send a signal. If it was Morse code, Donna was clueless. "Mother, you can talk now."

Cecilia exhaled audibly. "Boy! That was hard." She used her flattened hand to fan herself. "Do you think everything Clyde said was true?"

It was a reasonable inquiry. Probably one Mark and the other detectives were currently asking themselves. It might be as close to the truth as they'd ever get. Everyone had their own version of the truth. Depending on how they told it, they were either a hero or a victim. "Don't know. I'm sure Clyde is doing his best to look less guilty. If the designs were Cynthia's and she does have a life insurance policy on J.D., then it would give her the most motivation. It's all being checked out as I speak."

Her mother put the potato and peeler down. "That solves our missing tycoon issue. Good, because we have another matter that will require our immediate attention."

No, not another issue. Was there a rule she couldn't have an issue-free day at least once? Donna glanced into the bowl, calculating the amount of potatoes. Not nearly enough. She'd hear what her mother had to say, especially if she kept peeling.

"Tell me what little matter needs my attention." Donna took a deep breath and put down the paring knife to avoid an accident if she resorted to clenching her hands.

That's all her mother needed to hear. "Tennyson called."

Even though she may have complained about Tennyson, her

former helper, and his melancholy attitude, she certainly missed him. In his own way, he was family. It made her wonder why he called Cecilia and not her. "That's great. Is he coming for a visit?"

"In a way," Cecilia's lips turned up in a sly smile. "Turns out that Herman and Lola haven't made it to Vegas yet and are coming back for a visit. They were hoping you could arrange a little faux wedding ceremony for all the Legacy folks to attend. They thought you could say a few words in front of friends. They are still heading to Vegas for the legal wedding and all."

Oh, that's all.

Chapter Twenty-Three

ALL IT TOOK was the mention of a wedding that would be happening in twenty-four hours to turn a mellow, celebratory dinner preparation into absolute chaos. Donna peered into the bowl of diced potatoes with dismay. "We'd better make a lot more potatoes. I'll invite Maria and Daniel over for supper."

Her mother slid off the stool and started poking around the kitchen, pulling out drawers and opening cabinet doors. "I'll invite Simon and Heloise," she volunteered.

The very thought of the town gossip in her kitchen rehashing tidbits she'd embellished about the locals was enough to put Donna off her feed. "Not Heloise."

Her mother probably thought she was the fastest way to relay vital information to Herman's friends and associates. Trying to explain she could do without Heloise's sharp tongue would end up with her mother lecturing about charity and being nice to those who were less fortunate than her. She had to think of another reason. Being nice to others wasn't a hardship as long as it wasn't Heloise and there wasn't food involved, too.

"I don't have enough pork chops to go around. Besides, I'm sure she'll be at the wedding."

Cecilia stopped her rooting through her kitchen to glance back at her daughter. "You're right. Wild horses couldn't stop her from attending the wedding. It's probably just as well. She finds you a little abrasive."

"Me? Abrasive?" Donna was about to insist she was far from difficult to deal with but managed to rein her tongue in before she ended up inviting Heloise to supper just to prove she was all kindness and generosity. "What are you looking for anyhow?"

"Pen and paper. We need to make a list of what needs to be done."

Made sense. "Can't we just do what we did for my wedding? I'm sure the details are in Maria's laptop."

Her mother stopped her search and gave her daughter a long look. "You had a wedding planner."

"Not a real one. It was a ploy to find out who was killing all the other wedding planners. In the end, she did nothing. You, Maria, and Janice did all the work. Anyway, there are courtesy tablets and pens on the foyer table."

For a woman who was seventy plus, her mother could move. She nipped out into the hall and returned with pen and pad in two shakes of a lamb's tail. The pad hit the counter with a thud while Cecilia reached for her burbling phone. She pecked at the keyboard just like a millennial who had texting issues.

Potatoes had to be peeled and diced, plus Donna had more pork chops to thaw, along with planning and creating a wedding reception menu, but it didn't stop her from being curious. "Who are you texting?"

"Maria. We don't have time to chat on the phone."

That's something she'd expect a much younger person to say. If her mother managed to type the details of the impromptu wedding that quickly, she could count herself very impressed. "What did you say?"

"Emergency. Inn. Come quick." She pursed her lips. "I didn't say anything about bringing Daniel." Her shoulders went up in an *oh well* shrug. "He wouldn't be that much help planning, but he can move furniture later or pick up stuff."

"Whoa." Donna blew out a breath, thinking of Maria racing over to the inn certain there was either a hostage situation or major blood loss involved. "Tell me you didn't actually text that."

"I just told you I did. Weren't you paying attention?" Her mother resumed her seat and started writing. "I'm sure both Herman and his bride brought clothes for the wedding. We already have the venue. So, two things down. We will need a minister." She held up her index finger as she pondered the situation. "You used Herman for your wedding."

True, she had. "It's not like he's going to perform his own wedding. Besides, they are both from out-of-state. It would take almost two months to get a marriage license in North Carolina. No shotgun weddings here."

The information, instead of deflating her mother's determination to make the event happen, only caused her to grin. "Well, that solves one problem. I'll call up Buster Soames."

Good Heavens. Surely her mother must have taken a wrong mental turn. "Not the creepy clown guy."

"Calm down. Not too many people want clowns for birthday parties anymore. Due to all the stories and movies about murderous clowns, the demand is low. Buster is now a justice of the peace. He will travel anywhere and do weddings. He has done more than a few pretend weddings when the couple had eloped without giving the parents the satisfaction of seeing their progeny wed. Only this time, the actual wedding will take place after the fake one does. No one will care if it is legal or not except us, Buster, and of course, Herman and Lola."

It sounded like a workable solution and at twenty-three hours and some minutes left, she wasn't certain she could do much better. "Give him a call, but be clear it's *not* a clown event. No big shoes, or red nose, or crazy hair, or anything."

"On it." Her mother held up her phone. "You should know the hair is his own and the red nose is due to an overfondness for scotch."

Tenseness developed in Donna's shoulders, and she reminded herself to take deep breaths. Why would a wedding be so much more trouble than running an inn or solving a murder? One step at a time, and everything would fall into place. "Remind him if he isn't sober, he doesn't get paid, and we'll call my friend Janice to pinch-hit since she's a notary, which is *kind* of official."

Her mother didn't answer, too busy tapping out a number. If nothing else, Donna could finish food prep and then concentrate on what really mattered—wedding reception food. She might as well get out her laptop and put in a grocery order to be delivered. She wouldn't have time to shop.

Her mother's voice interrupted her food planning. "Heloise! I'm so glad I reached you."

Since Donna couldn't hear what was being said on the other end, she imagined various locals having their private lives examined until her mother spoke.

"I need Buster's cell number. I know you two have been keeping company."

The thought of the town's most notorious gossip and the creepy clown guy as a couple made her close her eyes for a second. Maybe it was true that there was someone for everyone.

"Heloise, you stop that right now! I'm not trying to make time with your guy. I want to hire him for an event...no, not that kind of event. A wedding."

There was silence from her mother, who was probably being peppered with questions. Did Heloise seriously think her mother was interested in Buster? Or was it just the woman's way of jumping to the worst conclusion. It was probably the latter. She tried not to eavesdrop, but it was hard with her mother sitting about three feet from her.

"Herman and his fiancée are going to be married at the inn. Tomorrow…no, it's not a hurry-up wedding. For Pete's sake, they're both in their eighties." There was more silence on her mother's side, and then she started writing something on the tablet. "Oh, okay. Put him on. Hi, Buster. I wonder if you are free to perform a wedding."

Donna rolled her eyes. Only Heloise would put someone on the spot before handing the phone over to whomever the person originally wanted to speak. Thankfully, Cecilia had more patience with stunts like that than Donna did. Maybe she'd become more tolerant and easier going as the years passed, but she had her doubts.

TEN MINUTES LATER, she had the potatoes in the skillet and opted for baked pork chops since they took less preparation. Donna had her computer booted up and was going through casual wedding receptions ideas. Vegetarian couscous salad was a no. Whole lobster accompanied by mac and cheese was another no. The reception would be hers and Mark's gift to the couple. It would be fitting since Herman was the first person in the neighborhood to befriend her.

A groan came from the side door hinges as it was wrenched open, and Maria, red-faced and breathless, ran into the kitchen and slowly turned around, glancing at the occupants. "Is it Mark? Jasper? Simon? What happened?"

Donna cut her eyes to her mother, who cleared her throat.

"Hope you didn't break any speed records getting here. Have a seat. We have a family emergency and need all hands-on deck, so to speak. We need to have a wedding of sorts here tomorrow."

"What?" More than a little irritation tainted her sister-in-law's voice. "I left Cici with a neighbor to rush over here. If someone wants to book a wedding, there's an application on the inn website they need to fill out. They can't snap their fingers and expect it to happen."

If Donna didn't know it was Herman and Lola—plus Tennyson probably suggested it, assuming all a person did was snap their fingers for flowers, food, and a minister to mysteriously appear—she'd be in full rant with Maria. "Herman wants a little do here with his friends. I assume he means our family since he moved to Indiana to be close to his war buddies. It shouldn't be too much trouble. They have the clothes. We have the venue. I can fix the food. Surely, we can pick up a cake at the local grocery and stick a wedding topper on it. Mother has already booked Buster Soames to officiate."

Maria rubbed her hand over her face, peeked between her fingers, and said, "Not creepy, birthday clown guy."

"He does weddings," Cecilia pointed out.

"Besides," Donna was quick to reassure her sister-in-law, "it's not about who officiates. It's for show, not legal and simply celebrating a solemn vow with friends."

"And a creepy, birthday clown guy." Maria propped her elbow on the island and rested her head in her hand.

Here, Donna thought she would be the naysayer of the bunch. She strolled over to Maria and patted her on the shoulder. "No worries. Buster won't be decked out in clown regalia, and he'll be sober. Right?" She nodded in her mother's direction.

"Absolutely," Cecilia confirmed with a nod. "I was hoping you would help with decorations and flowers. We need Daniel in the morning to help move stuff."

"Most of the guests usually check out after breakfast on Sunday. It'll be chaos with the guests checking out, food to cook, and rooms to be cleaned. Mark will still probably be at work assembling information on the case." Donna managed a weary smile at the thought of it. "At least I have Rosemarie to help, and she's pretty good with guests. If nothing else, she can turn the rooms and do the laundry."

Her mother coughed violently.

Donna slapped her on the back and asked, "Are you choking? Raise your hand if you are."

Her mother held up both hands and managed to gasp, "Not choking. Please don't Heimlich maneuver me." She inhaled audibly and shook her head. "I forgot to tell you. Rosemarie left."

No, she couldn't have. True, she hadn't seen any sign of the woman when she came back after her snooping adventure with Peanut. Still, her mother could have been confused. Rosemarie might have said she was going out for a while. A dash into the tiny room that served as the inn's staff bedroom was empty except for the twin bed and chest of drawers. It was Donna's turn to jog into the kitchen, red-faced and bug-eyed. "What happened?"

Her mother held a finger up to her lips, then dropped it. "Remember my saying I couldn't get Rosemarie to gossip about her family? Eventually, she broke and told me how her siblings weren't speaking to one another. Families can go to pieces with the death of a parent."

"What did you do, Mother?" All Donna knew was she didn't have any help when she needed it the most.

Her mother arched her eyebrows. "I reunited family. All it took was a caring third party and a threat of legal action. Rosemarie moved back into the house. The brother has agreed to quit bad-mouthing her or face being charged with slander. As a salesman, he'd rather not have that accusation attached to his name. Honestly, I believe he loves his sister. All's well."

How was all *well* if Donna had just lost her one employee? She didn't begrudge Rosemarie having the life she wanted, but she could have used another pair of hands. "All is *not* well." She put her fists on her hips. "I needed an assistant, which is the reason I put an ad in the paper."

Her mother giggled. "Don't take on so. I handled that, too." She glanced down at her delicate wristwatch. "Your new employee should be here soon. Just in time to help with the wedding plan-ning."

The sound of a wonky transmission and a squeal of worn brakes in the parking lot were very familiar. Donna had to check to see if the worst was true. A glance through the kitchen lace curtains revealed Thelma getting out with a duffle bag. At least she wasn't leading a herd of marauders disguised as apple-cheeked children.

Chapter Twenty-Four

B Y TEN P.M., Donna had decided on a traditional menu of fried chicken and mashed potatoes with country gravy. She considered corn on the cob but rejected it in favor of seasoned green beans. Who wanted corn stuck in their teeth, especially when wearing their wedding finery? "Oh!"

Maria, who sat hunched over the island weaving silk flowers around bowls that would be filled with water and one floating candle, glanced up. "I'm afraid to ask *what* this late when I'm sure there's nothing we can do."

Her sister-in-law was so right. Normally, she'd be tucked in bed with a mystery novel or enjoying a crime drama on television. "It's nothing. I just remembered I took that weekend course to marry folks. You remember? In case the inn became a wedding destination."

"Hmm," Maria worked her mouth one way, then another. "Yeah, that's right. You got some certificate or something."

"It's a license," Donna clarified. She didn't pay two hundred and fifty dollars for a certificate, along with two days of her life she'd never get back. Most of the seminar was spent trying to sell the participants on other things they might want to try, such as being a notary or an auctioneer. "Still, Mother did get Buster. I don't want to undermine her work."

"Ha!" Maria half-laughed. "Tell the truth. You don't want to upset Heloise. Who knows what rumor she'd start about you or the inn? Possibly bedbugs."

Donna rapped on top of the island to ward off such a thing. Her actions caused Thelma to stop writing out the place settings in careful calligraphy. Who knew the woman would have actual useful skills for weddings?

The woman glanced up with a serene expression. "Don't worry. Everything will work out as it should."

As predictions went, that was a safe one. Rather like their local weatherman predicting rain or not, he did with such good humor it was hard to resent being told absolutely nothing useful. Besides, the non-reports were a tradition in these parts. "Is that your opinion or a prediction?"

Thelma stared at the cat clock before answering. "Could be either."

Weariness weighed on Donna, but she managed to nod as opposed to replying. Were her days going to be filled with cryptic sayings that could be predictions or not? It reminded her of Tennyson. At least his utterances were of the philosophical nature and usually depressing until love entered the picture.

Too bad her mother had left before she could ask what she had been thinking to help one employee out the door and hire another one while Donna and Peanut were doing their best not to be shot. Her mother would answer that she was only helping out, which would be true. If only she had consulted Donna before going full steam on whatever plan seemed perfect to Cecilia. It was hard to remember exactly, but Donna remembered Tennyson made a similar comment about her.

"I think you two should call it a night. The morning will come soon enough. Go on." She flipped her hands in a shooing motion.

When Maria started picking up the loose silk flower chains, Donna shook her head. "I'll get this since I'll still be waiting up for Mark to hear what happened."

Both Thelma and Maria promised to be back bright and early. Little did Thelma know that being next to the kitchen, she'd hear Donna starting breakfast. Tennyson used to gripe that she banged pans around to make certain he was awake. Yeah, she did do that.

Once the women left, the kitchen felt empty, and the silence hung heavily except for Jasper snoring and the click of the cat clock tail. Donna tidied up the area, put on a pot of decaf coffee, and made a sandwich for her husband, who should be walking through the door soon. She might not have Thelma's psychic skills, but she did know Mark should have been home hours ago. With the murderers in jail and J.D. in the morgue, what else was there to do?

The side door creaked open. Jasper opened one eye while he struggled into a sitting position. His tail wagged, letting Donna know he recognized her hubby's footsteps. "Hush." She addressed Jasper, knowing he normally barked when Mark arrived home. Instead of guard dog behavior, it was more a joyous homecoming for the man who offered pizza crusts, French fries, and who knew what else to her pooch. "There's probably at least one person sleeping who thinks dogs don't belong in the inn. Never mind that it's our home."

Mark entered the kitchen and sniffed the air. "Decaf, I assume."

"You know it." She retrieved the plate with the sandwich from the counter and placed it on the island.

"Thanks, honey. I may be too tired to eat." He dropped onto a stool with a groan. "What a night."

"Tell me about it," Donna prompted as she poured a cup of coffee. Mainly she'd been waiting for the lowdown on the case, but she also felt her husband shouldn't come home to no one waiting up for him. He had done that for three decades. When she placed the cup in front of Mark, he was eating.

"Thanks," he said through a half-full mouth. He picked up the coffee and sipped. Most people would have blown on it. Years of drinking the sludge at the station that passed for coffee must have made him immune to burning liquid. "That Cynthia is a piece of work."

"How so?" Donna took a seat on the stool across from Mark.

He sighed, took another bite, and chewed slowly. "I'm very grateful you're alive." He reached across the island to cover Donna's hand with his own. "Most folks we bring in who are guilty of killing someone reacted in a moment of fear, stress, or were under the influence of drugs or alcohol. Many are just as shocked as everyone else that someone died because of their actions. This chick planned out J.D.'s death for years. Everyone she met was just a rung in getting closer to killing the man."

"Did she actually say that?"

While most killers confess readily on television shows, she always thought it would be stupid to do so. She knew the police had a variety of psychological games to get a person to talk, such as sympathizing with the perp, but Cynthia would have seen through it.

"In a way. At first, she insisted she did nothing wrong." Mark grimaced and took another sip of coffee. "We hit her with criminal trespass, assault, assault on an officer, having an unlicensed gun and silencer, interfering with police procedure, then finally premeditated murder. She kept sticking her nose up in the air as if everything was laughable, then said J.D. deserved to die considering how he treated her. She was only sorry J.D. was dead because he couldn't be punished as he was the *real* criminal. She used her phone call to bring Eugenia to the station."

While she'd missed out on that information, she had wondered how cousin Eugenia fit into everything. "How'd that go?"

"Personally, I was thrilled she showed up." He waggled his eyebrows and smirked. "Saved us time. We put the two of them into a room to talk, then we listened. Not sure why anyone would think a room in a police station wouldn't be wired for sound."

"Not admissible in court," she reminded.

"True, but it's a way to get useful information. Anyhow, Cynthia was pressing her cousin to say they'd spent every moment together. She was to be the alibi. Eugenia wasn't having it and complained that she was sorry she had even agreed to accompany her on the trip. Even though it may seem like Eugenia's the dominant one in the relationship, it didn't sound like that. Apparently, Cynthia egged Eugenia on to call the police when you were locked out of the house. I can only assume she wanted to keep you busy. Cynthia has a lot of brass."

"You got enough to convict?" Guilty people often slip the restraints of justice due to a lack of evidence or the ability to charm a jury.

Mark held up a thumb. "Neil, our computer guy, managed to locate the insurance claim. Guess what?" Before she could reply, her hubby continued, "Cynthia had the policy increased to three million. She'd been boosting the payout all along. Not sure who her agent was, allowing her to do it without talking to J.D." His shoulders went up in a shrug. "She could have paid someone to pretend to be J.D., though. Insurance companies aren't fond of paying out that kind of money. Even if Cynthia had got away with it, she'd be tied up trying to get her funds."

"That explains how she thought she'd end up rich, when it was obvious, she couldn't inherit. That's good. I can go to bed without worrying about that. Now all I have to do is concentrate on the wedding."

"The what?"

Oh, right. Her husband had missed out on the latest development.

★

THE DAY STARTED before dawn with Donna eyeing the front parlor, trying to decide if they should use the bridal arch and how many chairs to set up. Even though she didn't expect many to attend, it was better to have too many chairs than not enough. She made some mental calculations before making breakfast.

A shaft of light showed underneath the door, proving someone had beat her to the kitchen. The last thing she needed was a guest fixing their own breakfast. Whoever it was would soon discover she had the fridge, most of the cupboards, and her basement, which served as a wine cellar, locked up tight due to previous midnight snackers.

With her hand flat on the door, she pushed it open a couple of inches to reveal Thelma talking to Jasper.

"Now that you've had your morning walk, I bet you'd like breakfast."

The dog stared up at his new best friend and wagged his tail. Goodness, Thelma had taken the dog for a walk already.

When Jasper turned his head toward Donna, Thelma did likewise and spoke in a cheery tone "Good morning!"

Good gravy! Thelma was a morning person. She should have expected it. "Ah, morning. What are you doing up so early?"

"Lots to do," Thelma's eyebrows arched at the notion. "Besides, the morning is the best part of the day. I turned the oven on four hundred to preheat for the frittata."

Donna blinked. Maybe she had underestimated Thelma's psychic skills after all. "Did you have a feeling about this?"

"A what?" Forehead puckered, Thelma rubbed the back of her neck. "Not sure what you mean."

"The oven." Donna felt reluctant to say anymore because she already felt silly. "You know, four hundred degrees."

"Oh, that. I made the menus last night for this morning. I knew four hundred was the usual temperature to cook a frittata."

"You're right." Donna was unwilling to confess she thought the woman had used psychic skills to know what to set the oven to. "All right, we have our work cut out for us."

The two of them worked well together, getting out the food to the various guests. Maria showed with husband and child in tow. Daniel and Mark set out arranging the front parlor while Maria checked out guests and Thelma cleaned the rooms. By the time she'd finished the breakfast dishes, it was time to start the chicken she had soaking in brine all night. The front doorbell jingled and familiar voices sounded in the hallway. Donna darted out of the kitchen.

A grinning Herman had his arm around Lola as he conversed with Mark. Tennyson and his sweetheart, Sloane, were right behind them.

Sloane waved and shouted over the men, "I'm here to help!"

Maria snatched up Sloane before she could be sucked into kitchen detail. Fortunately, Thelma chose to take a break from room cleaning to help with the food. She smiled at Lola and pointed upstairs. "Look for an open door on the second floor to change."

Lola thanked her and turned to Herman. "I may need assistance in getting up there. I may have wanted to do this without my walker, but I will need help with the steps."

"No problem," Mark said and offered his arm with a flourish. "We have an elevator. What bag do you need?"

"The floral one." She pointed to a large fabric bag Tennyson had brought in.

While Mark escorted Lola to the room, Thelma sat down at the island and started to peel potatoes. "Do you have another bag?"

Donna pivoted and blinked a couple of times. "Why?"

"Just a feeling that there's going to be quite a few folks to wish Herman well."

That made sense. While Herman might not feel he had many friends his age in town, there were plenty of folks who respected him and who might take the opportunity to drop by, especially with Heloise manning the gossip hotline. Some might visit just to see if there was any truth in what the gossip was peddling. With that in mind, she needed to remind Daniel to pick up the cake.

"I'll be right back." Donna found her brother standing with Tennyson, Herman, and Mark, gabbing. *Typical.* The men talked while the women worked, but to be fair, the parlor looked grand. Donna stared at the men which had the result of them turning to her expectantly, waiting for orders.

"You," she pointed to her brother, "need to get the cake. You might need to pick up an extra cake if they have one. Thelma seems to think we'll have more guests than expected."

She smiled sweetly at her husband. "See if you can find any champagne in the cellar. I know we have some."

Tennyson smirked at her, expecting a similar command. Before she could manufacture a task, Sloane called from the dining room, "Tenny, I need your help!"

"Herman," she addressed her former neighbor with a wink. "I need you to come into the kitchen to drink coffee and tell me what you've been up to."

He chuckled and followed Donna into the kitchen. Everything was falling into place. What seemed like an impossibility yesterday was becoming a reality today.

Epilogue

DONNA, DRESSED IN the gold and green dress she wore for her own wedding, kept her finger inserted into the small book for a traditional wedding ceremony. She hadn't planned for this. Who knew Buster would get a better offer in another county for a huge children's party? It was no wonder he was struggling with bookings if this was how he handled business. At least that was the excuse Heloise gave. Her mother pantomimed drinking. Whatever it was, he wasn't here. It seemed like everyone else was, though.

Thank goodness she had listened to Thelma and made extra food. The bedroom door opened, and Mark stuck his head in. "Hey, hon. You about ready?"

"Yes. It will be my first wedding I have conducted."

"No pressure. Remember, this one is for show. I think an Elvis impersonator is doing the one in Vegas. Herman's friends are here from the center."

"Oh no!" Donna pressed her hand against her chest, remembering what happened the last time they decided to make a road trip. "Should we call the home?"

"It's above board this time. Eunice's daughter drove them, which I assume was at a sedate speed, too." He continued. "Everyone is ready. Now, it's all you." Mark beamed at her and offered his bent arm.

"It's not all me, but thanks for saying so. I guess I'm surprised at how much change Herman experienced in his life. From what he told me, he had lived in the house across the street for almost his whole life. When he came back from the war to find his sweetheart hadn't waited for him, he assumed he'd be lonely the rest of his life. Then, he chose to move to Indiana, became a senior sleuth, fell in love, and now he and Lola are heading to Vegas."

Mark patted her hand that was tucked into the crook of his arm. "Who knew Herman would turn out to be the most adventurous?"

"Ah, I still have a lot of life left in me."

"How well I know."

"Still," she inhaled deeply. "Everything keeps changing."

"It's inevitable. You've changed."

"Me?" The idea surprised Donna. "How?"

"The Donna I met when I came to investigate the dead body in your second-best parlor would not be marrying folks."

"Well, I don't know—"

"I'm not finished."

"Go on."

"You wouldn't have taken a chance on love *or* me."

"I always thought you were cute, in a rumpled Columbo sort of way."

He laughed as he guided her to the front parlor where she took her place. A slight nod had Tennyson turning on the music. Elvis crooned about fools falling in love.

Herman pushed back his shoulders and glowed as Lola, escorted by Mark, moved slowly toward him. The bride was attired in a white lace pantsuit and a tiny matching hat that rested on top of her curls.

A tear threatened to slip down Donna's cheek as she watched the progress of the two coming up the aisle, remembering her husband's words. She had changed, taken chances, and look at the results.

Donna lifted the book only to realize she lost her place. Ah, she'd have to wing it. In that, some things never change.

THE END

Regatta Recipes

Easy Shortbread Cookies

Use the best butter you can afford.

Yield:
2 dozen

Ingredients

2 c. softened butter

1 c. white sugar

2 tsp. vanilla extract

4 cups all-purpose flour

Directions

1. Preheat oven to 350 degrees F (180 degrees C).
2. Cream butter and sugar until fluffy. Stir in vanilla; add flour and mix well.
3. Put through cookie press and form cookies onto baking sheets. Bake for 10 – 12 minutes.

Crunchy Fried Chicken

Yield: 16 pieces

Ingredients:
(2) whole chickens
Vegetable oil of choice, for frying the chicken
6 c. all-purpose flour
5 Tbsp salt
4 Tbsp ground black pepper
2 Tbsp garlic powder
1 Tbsp onion powder
2 tsp cayenne pepper
2 c. buttermilk

Directions

1. Cut the whole chickens into 4 breasts, 4 thighs, 4 legs and 4 wings and set aside. Place chicken into salt water in a sealed container and place in fridge overnight.
2. Next day: drain water and pat chicken parts dry.
3. Preheat your oil, in either a heavy pan on the stove or a deep-fryer, to 325 degrees.
4. In a large bowl, combine the flour, salt, black pepper, garlic powder, onion powder and cayenne pepper until thoroughly mixed. Set aside.
5. Pour the buttermilk into another bowl large enough for the chicken to be immersed in the buttermilk.
6. Prepare your dredging station. Place your chicken in a bowl. Next to that, your bowl of buttermilk, and next to that, your dry mixture.
7. Take your breasts, lightly dust them with your flour mixture, then dip them in the buttermilk until they are coated, and then place them in the flour mixture. Take the breasts that are in the flour mixture and aggressively push the flour mixture into the wet chicken. Make sure that the chicken in very thoroughly coated, or you will not achieve the crust and crunch you are looking for. Gently place the breasts in your hot oil.

8. Next, repeat the dredging steps with your other pieces of chicken in this order: thigh, leg then wing. When you place the last wing into the fryer, you should have 16 pieces of chicken in the oil. Set a timer for 15 minutes.
9. After 15 minutes, take a probe thermometer and check the temperature of a breast. If it reads 180 degrees F, all of your chicken is done. (Keep in mind that it will continue to cook after it has been removed from the fryer.)
10. Remove the chicken from the oil and let it drain for 5 minutes. Let cool for an additional 10 minutes before serving.

Makes for excellent leftovers, too.

Seasoned Green Beans

Ingredients
1 lb. of fresh, green beans
½ cup of finely chopped white onion
1 garlic clove
2 strips of wide cut bacon
1-2 cups of chicken broth
1 Tablespoon of butter
1 teaspoon of red pepper flakes
Seasoning salt & black pepper to taste.

Directions
1. Wash the green beans.
2. Snap off the ends of the greens beans and cut or snap the green beans into pieces. Set aside.
3. Finely dice onion, garlic, and bacon. Set aside.
4. In a saucepan or pot, melt butter.
5. Add in onion, garlic, bacon and chicken broth.
6. Bring to a boil and add in red pepper flakes
7. Add in green beans.
8. Cover and simmer for 1-1½ hours. Check the green beans every 5 minutes after the one-hour mark. You don't want to overcook.
9. Season with seasoning salt & black pepper.
10. Serve.

Mashed Potatoes

Simple and delicious

Ingredients

2 pounds baking potatoes, peeled and quartered
2 tablespoons butter
1 cup milk
salt and pepper to taste

Directions

Bring a pot of salted water to a boil. Add potatoes and cook until tender but still firm, about 15 minutes; drain.

In a small saucepan heat butter and milk over low heat until butter is melted. Using a potato masher or electric beater, slowly blend milk mixture into potatoes until smooth and creamy. Season with salt and pepper to taste.

Country Gravy

Ingredients
1/2 c vegetable oil **or** 6 1/3 Tbsp of melted butter (not both)
3/4 c all-purpose flour
1 tsp salt
1 tsp ground black pepper
4 c milk

Directions
1. Heat the oil in a large skillet over medium heat.
2. Whisk in the flour, salt and pepper until smooth.
3. Cook and stir over medium heat until browned, about 10 minutes.
4. Gradually stir in milk so that no lumps form, and continue cooking and stirring until thick.
5. If the gravy becomes too thick, you may thin it with a little more milk.

Late for Square Dancing

Chapter One

E VEN THOUGH THE trees had cast off their autumn finery, the sun still shone bright and there wasn't even a hint of approaching winter in the air. The unexpected warm stretch had lured people outside with mothers pushing strollers and kids riding bikes. Even a few folks were out cutting grass. At the head of the neighborhood where Greener Pastures Convalescent Center stood, the parking lot was full, but the only person spotted outside was a nurse's aide half-hidden in the building's shadow, furtively smoking a cigarette next to the no smoking sign.

Loud music poured from the doorway another employee pushed open as she left. There was a shout of *do-si-do!* before the door swung shut. The departing employee waved at the smoker, then headed for her car at a jog as if eager to leave. Inside the center, however, the pace of the day differed.

The sounds of clicking, music, and a man who occasionally called out random commands, such as bow to your corner or bow to your partner, filled the corridors surrounding the large dining room. Inside the room, residents were crowded so closely together that it wouldn't be a surprise if their wheelchair wheels got entangled.

At a table closest to the door, three people sat: a short, bald man, and two women. The first had her blonde hair arranged in an elaborate style and lacquered into place by a liberal dose of hair spray. She winced a little but had her head tilted in the direction of a wiry woman whose lips were moving.

"This is how it works, Lola," the woman explained while gesturing to the dancers. "The man calls out the moves for the dancers, then they have to do what he tells them to do."

"Eunice," Lola sighed and managed an eye roll at the same time, "I know how square-dancing works. This isn't my first encounter, you know."

"Ha!" Eunice tossed her head, bouncing her gray-threaded curls. "I figured that being a former Vegas showgirl, your extent of dancing involved teetering around on high heels, waving feather fans."

The man sitting with them coughed, earning a sympathetic glance from Lola. "You okay, Gus? Need some water?"

He met her gaze, then shook his head as he pushed up to standing. "Think I'll go back to my room and get some water."

Both women watched Gus leave, then Eunice leaned closer to say, "He has no clue what you said. He's already hard of hearing, but with…" She gestured to a nearby speaker. "…the music blasting, he doesn't hear a word."

While the music may have a few residents tapping their toes, it did nothing for those who *could* hear. Lola pursed her lips and wrinkled her nose before speaking. "You'd think they're trying to deafen the rest of us. I'm leaving, too." Lola reached for her walker and stood. She glanced back over her shoulder to address Eunice's earlier comment. "Showgirl routines are choreographed. Some of it is quite complicated. We certainly never needed someone yelling instructions on a microphone."

Eunice gave a derisive sniff. Even though both she and Lola were part of Senior Sleuths, a covert group within the center that solved cold cases, it was still fun to poke at the woman. After all, what woman wouldn't feel a little uncomfortable around a former showgirl. Getting the aged blonde riled up evened the playing field, especially considering Eunice's skinny form and acerbic nature didn't make her popular with the opposite gender. Thank goodness for Gus, who had been waiting for a forceful woman to take charge of him.

Making friends was not something Eunice did easily. Her father once told her she should laugh at the other children's jokes and occasionally compliment them on something they did. He also told her to be honest at all times. Talk about a paradox. It was hard to be honest and popular. Eventually, she settled on being honest and helpful, even when the help wasn't wanted. Was it too late to change her ways? Better yet, did she want to?

One of the lady dancers, whose colorful skirt stood out with its multitude of petticoats, interrupted Eunice's reflections and invited her to join in. Someone had deliberately picked her. Woo hoo! She jumped up and tried to ignore that most of the other attendees were in wheelchairs. That had nothing to do with them picking her. Obviously, the dancer recognized in Eunice a born square dancer.

The dancer had a firm grip on Eunice's arm as if afraid she might fall and guided her through the steps. Opposite of them were a few other residents being herded in a similar manner. Such behavior might be expected for one of the more confused residents, but Eunice didn't need that type of treatment and shook off her helping hand. "I can follow directions," she shouted to her helper, who smiled back with an apologetic grin.

By keeping an eye on the dancer in front of her, Eunice mim-icked the moves, albeit a few seconds late, which made her a little bit out of step. Of course, if she knew what the commands meant, she'd be golden. If the home had lessons, instead of randomly bringing in a group to demonstrate, then she'd be all over it. That was the problem with the center's activities director. She trotted people in to demonstrate, assuming that everyone was so old they'd never want to do something on their own.

The previous shuffleboard tournament had been a result of constant complaining about endless bingo, which had been the sum of their activities. One tournament, while fun, did not change the daily bingo games. The rumor was the occasional church handbell choir or scout troop that showed up came by choice and were not solicited by the director. Even this group was associated with the receptionist, who stood on the sidelines, clapping. Eunice blinked when she noticed the dancers had formed two lines, leaving her stranded in the middle. It must be a dance circle. Time to be the spotlight dancer. She placed her hands on her hips and placed one foot out while trying to recall the tap lessons she had taken as a kid. Nothing was coming. The original dancer who had invited her to dance was waving wildly at her, then pointing to the line.

Ah, it might not be a dance circle. Just as well, since no moves had filtered back into her mind over the years. The sizable bulk of Herman, another Senior Sleuth, filled the doorway. He, too, was waving, but not necessarily in the panicky way of the dancer. He must be trying to rescue her, bless him.

She gave the line of dancers and the seated residents a hand wave worthy of the queen. "Pressing business. I must go. Carry on."

A few curious looks, muttered comments, and a lone laugh followed Eunice as she weaved her way through the people. Even though she was tempted to swing around to see who might be laughing at her, she didn't. She kept her head high and her back straight and moved toward the door.

Herman urged her out of the main room, away from the speakers. Music filtered into the hallway but faded as they strolled away from the dining room and turned into one of the adjoining corridors before trying to speak. Finally, Eunice nudged Herman with her elbow and asked, "What's up?"

Herman reached up to stroke his handlebar mustache, which was his newest affectation, and replied, "Lance is here. Marci told me to round up the sleuths."

While it might not have sounded like much to anyone who cared to eavesdrop, it pretty much summed up the situation. Marci was a detective who had been severely injured in the line of duty. A car crash that shattered her leg, along with being shot more than once, had placed her in the home, fighting to recover simple acts, such as walking. While her body was recuperating, her old partner brought her cold cases to solve. In an act of compassion, she had invited select residents to help her solve the cases. Her rationale was that some of the cases were old, and locals would know the politics and streets of days gone by.

Eunice had not been invited to join, but she was as sharp as any of them. After all, she knew they were sneaking out. It wasn't all that hard to miss Gus's bald pate or his tendency to shout everything since his hearing was impaired due to being an explosives specialist in the army. Some might call it underhanded, but she basically blackmailed her way into the group. They needed her but hadn't recognized it yet.

"Ah, a new case. About time." She rubbed her hands together. "We could use something to liven up this place."

Author Notes

The Painted Lady Inn Mysteries series is my first cozy mystery series. Most authors spend time insisting that their characters have nothing to do with actual real people. Not so with my characters, Donna, my main character, has a great bit of my mother in her. My mother was a registered nurse who worked at a hospital, then went on to be a visiting nurse and also worked for the Red Cross. Much of Donna's germ phobia plus professional insights into the nursing field are via my mother. Donna's practicality along with her thriftiness was courtesy of my grandmother who was a young window who had to raise four children while making ends meet.

The culinary aspects are courtesy of my grandmother plus my own experiences. My grandmother taught herself to cook and became quite well known for her baked creations. This talent kept her family fed since she spent her early morning hours at a bakery making bread, cookies, donuts, and pies for the day. I on the other hand worked in dietary at a local nursing home where I sometimes cooked for three hundred plus people. It became a running joke that I couldn't make anything for less than a hundred folks.

The character of Mark has some of the same traits as my own husband plus a handful from 1970s television sleuths. As for Jasper, he was a mirror image of my old dog, Chance, only a little smaller.

The rest of the folks are mostly works of fiction. Overheard conversations, odd news stories, and even day dreaming helped create the guests and townspeople. That sums up the denizens of Legacy. Let's move on to my everyday life.

Usually I balance my week out with writing, reading and volunteering at the local Humane Society. Hobbies include making jewelry and gardening depending on the season. Due to our recent health crisis, I will not be making any personal appearances at this time. In the meantime, stay in touch via my newsletter. Sign up at www.morgankwyatt.com.

Subscribers find out about exclusive freebies, contests, and personal appearances.

If you feel like writing a review, please do.

Reading takes you to your happy place. We need happy moments now more than ever.

MK Scott

www.morgankwyatt.com

www.ingramcontent.com/pod-product-compliance
Lightning Source LLC
Chambersburg PA
CBHW050845180626
46814CB00007B/2630

* 9 7 8 1 9 4 4 7 1 2 6 2 4 *